HEROES AND LEGENDS

WIZARDS

BY DAVID AND LESLEY McINTEE
ILLUSTRATED BY MARK STACEY

ROSEN
PUBLISHING

New York

This edition published in 2016 by:
The Rosen Publishing Group, Inc.
29 East 21st Street
New York, NY 10010

Library of Congress Cataloging-in-Publication Date

McIntee, David A., author.
Wizards/David and Lesley McIntee.
    pages cm.—d(Heroes and legends)
Reprint of: Oxford, UK ; Long Island City, NY: Osprey Publishing, 2014.
Includes bibliographical references and index.
ISBN 978-1-4994-6176-3 (library bound)
1. Wizards—dHistory. I. McIntee, Lesley, author. II. Title.
BF1589.M48 2015
133.4'309—dc23

2014050281

Manufactured in the United States of America

© 2016 Osprey Publishing Limited
First published in paperback by Osprey Publishing Limited

CONTENTS

INTRODUCTION

A belief in magic has always existed. In the earliest societies, shamans tried to establish control over nature in order to help their communities survive. Some tried to propitiate the gods, starting religions, while others tried to replicate natural effects. The shaman was believed to maintain the balance between man and nature, to travel to other realms, and to transform himself into animal form.

As civilization developed, the purpose of magic changed. It became an expression of greed for knowledge, power, or money. Sometimes it became a weapon. The best intentions, like the desire for wisdom, were seen afterwards as bad deeds. Knowledge was a dangerous thing in times of scientific ignorance or religious extremism. "Magus" was a term of respect in the Near East for a learned man, but if you earned the reputation of being a "sorcerer" in the European Middle Ages, you were in serious trouble. Such accusations were convenient political tools for enemies of some of those who appear in this book.

Whether there really were people who could use words to change themselves into animals, fly through the air, summon devils, or turn lead into gold, one thing is certain – wizards and their talents have always been a popular subject for entertainment.

Many of their tales share similar tropes. Academic Elsie Butler concluded that there is a universal "myth of the magus," with very distinct and recognizable elements. It usually starts with the wizard's strange childhood—they might be fostered, or show magical powers from birth or around puberty. Harry Potter was lucky as most wizards of myth and legend did not have an easily accessed education. They had to travel far and wide to gain their knowledge and were often outcasts.

For some wizards of legend, there is a period of wandering in an inhospitable environment, while others were apprenticed to an existing wizard to be formally taught their craft. All of the great magi of legend underwent tests, trials, or temptations to prove their worth. They would have a formal initiation, which marked them out as different to their fellow men and invested them with some form of authority, even if only within a clandestine group. One of these tests is a magical duel to the death with another wizard, and a number of legends suggest the apparent death and rebirth of the wizard as part of the ongoing learning process. The experience of death allowed the wizard to communicate with spirits.

(OPPOSITE)
Throughout history, wizards have worked in their magic circles to conjure spirits or demons and to acquire power or knowledge, as in this 19th-century painting. (North Wind Picture Archive / Alamy)

By the end of their lives, it was imperative that they find someone worthy of receiving their knowledge and carrying on their work. So, where we find a wizard we usually find an apprentice or two. One of the most famous magical books, the *Sworn Book of Honorius*, made its keeper promise to make three copies only before his death, to pass to his successors.

Some of these stories might seem familiar to us from their very recent retellings: the wizard as a young boy, discovering his talents; magical books that have a tendency to develop a life of their own and may need to be chained down; arcane languages, alphabets, and words like "Expelliarmus!" or "Abracadabra!" or "Stercus stercus moriturus sum."

From behind the friendly face of the old grey-bearded wizard still peeps the shaman in his skins and hides, half-man, half-beast, lost in the mists of prehistoric time; the alchemist in his smoke-filled den, risking death by explosion as he mixes his impossible elixirs; the scholar, hiding his thoughts in code. Behind all of those shifting faces and identities, the trickster god of the old pagan world stretches out his hand to grant universal truth, but only if it is earned through hard work and even then at a price.

The Brothers Grimm should have the last word, though. In 1816 they wrote, "The stories of witches and wizards have survived better—and will survive better than any others—as our superstitious minds expect a better tale of good and evil from a wizard than they would from a giant or dwarf, which is why these are the only tales of the people that are welcome also among the educated classes."

THE ORIGINAL WIZARDS

Dedi – The Ancient Egyptian Sorcerer

The pharaoh, Khufu, was bored. Work was going well on the gigantic pyramid and on the remodelling of the Sphinx's face to match his own, but the day was too hot to be working on these construction projects, so the pharaoh wanted entertainment. His advisors suggested that he go fishing, so Khufu boarded his royal barge, powered by both sail and 20 women rowers. The rowers thought it amusing to wear dresses made of faience glass beads, resembling fishing nets. This pleased Khufu, who, carrying a gold fishing rod, was torn between trying to catch his rowers or actual fish.

Neither were biting. It would take a miracle to cheer up the pharaoh, and that was what he wanted. His son, Prince Djedef-hor, said, "There is a miracle worker, a commoner named Dedi, who lives in the village of Djed-Snefru. He is 110 years old, and every day he eats 500 loaves of bread and a shoulder of beef, and drinks 100 jars of beer. He knows how to mend a severed head. He can make a lion walk behind him with no leash, and he knows the number of chambers in the sanctuary of Thoth." The sanctuary of Thoth was the tomb of the god who had brought the knowledge of magic to the world, and Khufu had long sought to add a replica to his list of building works. Excited, he dispatched the Prince to bring Dedi to the court.

Djedef-hor took a boat south to Djed-Snefru and then was carried in a golden litter to the house of an old man in a shabby loincloth.

"Greetings, oh blessed one," said the prince. "I have come to summon you by order of my father the king, Khufu. He will lead you through a good lifetime and to your ancestors who are in the necropolis."

Dedi replied with a smile, "Welcome, Prince Djedef-hor, who is beloved of his father. Unfortunately, I'm just an old man, unfit to travel all the way to the royal court."

He did not seem overly impressed that the pharaoh himself had summoned him. The prince didn't dare to threaten him in case his magic was as powerful as the pharaoh hoped, so instead he filled his head with promises.

"You will eat delicacies provided by the king, the food of his companions." Lured by these bribes, the old man gave in.

The Sphinx in the 19th century. The face was originally that of a lion but was remodeled into that of Khufu during his reign. (Library of Congress)

The prince's entourage went to the jetty and was stunned to see Dedi preparing two majestic ships. One ship, Dedi explained, was for himself, while the other one was for his books of magic, his servants, and his apprentices.

When the prince finally brought Dedi before his father, Khufu was unimpressed. How, he wondered, was this scruffy peasant supposed to perform miracles for his guests?

Khufu said, "Why is it that I have not seen you before?"

The old wizard answered, "Summon me and, look, I have come."

Then one of Dedi's students opened a box made of ebony and electrum, and handed him a wax model of a crocodile.

"Have you heard the tale of the wizard whose wife committed adultery?" As he spoke, Dedi placed the wax crocodile into the decorative pool in the center of the courtyard.

"It was in the time of my forefather, Nebka," Dedi said. "A maid saw the wizard's wife dallying in the pavilion by the garden pool with a villager. And the maid told the wizard's caretaker, who told the wizard. So, the wizard gave his caretaker a crocodile made of wax, just like this one," Dedi indicated the wax crocodile he had just placed in the water, "and instructed him to place it in the garden pool. The next time the villager arrived to be with the wizards wife…" Dedi snapped his fingers, and suddenly the wax crocodile in the royal pool thrashed its tail, rearing as it swelled to the size of a fully-grown Nile crocodile. As the assembled court drew back in shock, the now very real beast opened its snaggle-toothed jaws. "The beast devoured the wife's lover. Swallowed him whole in one gulp!" The crocodile in the royal pool thrashed in the water, hissing at the terrified spectators. Dedi approached the snarling reptile, and, to everyone's amazement, grabbed it in his arms.

He squeezed and crushed it until he held a wax crocodile again, which he put back in its box. Most of the court were already convinced that Dedi was a magnificent sorcerer. Khufu, though, was still unimpressed. He wanted to see a real miracle, and nothing less than life and death would suffice.

Remembering what his son had said, Khufu asked, "Is it true that you know how to mend a severed head?"

Dedi nodded. Khufu said, "Bring forth a condemned man, and let his sentence be executed." Dedi refused immediately, saying that performing such acts on people for entertainment was against the laws of the gods and the priesthood. Instead, he had a duck's head cut off by an apprentice. The body was placed on the west side of the audience hall and the head on the east side. Dedi incanted magic words, and suddenly the duck stood up and began to waddle across the floor. Its head began to roll towards it. Once the head had reached the body, the duck bent down to allow the head to remount the body. Then it stood up, quacking.

Astonished, Khufu had a goose brought to him, and the same trick was performed with it. He then had a sacrificial bull brought to him, and its head was cut off. Once again Dedi said his magic words, the head and body moved to meet behind him, and the bull stood whole once more.

Now the pharaoh was impressed. He invited Dedi for a more private audience and the promised feast. In his private apartments, Khufu said, "It is said that you know the number of chambers in the sanctuary of Thoth."

Dedi thought carefully. "I do not know the number, but I know where they are kept. There is a box of flint, in a room called "The Inventory," in Heliopolis. The sanctuary of Thoth is in that box."

"Will you go to Heliopolis for me and fetch this flint box?"

"No. I physically could not do that."

"But you are the greatest wizard in the world," Khufu exclaimed in disbelief. "I have just watched you conquer death itself. How can there be anything you cannot do?"

Dedi said, "Because it is already written that the sanctuary will be brought to you by the eldest of the three kings who are in the womb of Reddjedet. She is the wife of a priest of Ra, the Lord of Sakhbu. They will rule in the whole of this land, and the eldest will become chief priest at Heliopolis."

The pharaoh didn't want to hear any more, frustrated at being outmaneuvered by a prophecy.

"What is this mood, my lord?" Dedi asked him. "Was it caused by these children I mentioned?"

Khufu nodded. "When will Reddjedet give birth?"

"On the 15th day of the first month of Peret, when the sand banks of Two-Fish Canal are cut off. I will let four cubits of water appear there, so that you may attend the birth."

Then Khufu ordered that Dedi be assigned as the palace magician of Prince Djedef-hor, and that he should be paid with 1,000 loaves of bread, 100 jugs of beer, one ox, and 100 bunches of vegetables.

Soon, Reddjedet gave birth to three sons. Several of the gods had to help with a difficult labor, but the three princes were born healthy, and one of them did fulfill the prophecy. But that is another story.

The god Thoth, seen here in his Ibis-headed form, was believed to have brought knowledge of both magic and writing to mankind. Legend held that his dimensionally-transcendental tomb contained even more secrets of the gods. (Franck Camhi / Alamy)

The Historical Dedi and Ancient Egyptian Magic

Ninteenth-century scholars translated Dedi's tales from the sadly incomplete Westcar Papyrus. The first story in it is about the legendary builder and engineer, Imhotep, who is now better known as a wizard himself in *The Mummy* films. The wizard who uses the wax crocodile to remove his wife's lover is called Uba-in-er in the papyrus, which was written in the Hyksos period, sometime around 1600 BC. The stories themselves are oral traditions of the Middle Kingdom, a couple of centuries earlier, and are set during the Fourth Dynasty, *c.*2500 BC.

The ancient Egyptians wrote the earliest tales of what we would now call wizards, and Dedi is still considered by stage magicians to be the earliest conjuror. His trick of reattaching a severed bird head was still performed through the late 20th century until animal rights put an end to it. Dedi's story includes several firsts: control of animals, changing the scale of objects, apprentices, unusual longevity, and the association of wizards with book collecting.

The Egyptians believed in a power called "heka," which archaeologists translate as "magic," but is more accurately a sort of potential energy all around them, a bit like the Force in *Star Wars*. Magic was also present in writing, thanks to Thoth, and so the Egyptians wrote spells. To the Egyptians, an image and the object it portrayed were the same, and Egypt itself was full of dangerous animals: hippopotami, cobras, crocodiles, etc. So the ordinary ancient Egyptians bought or made images of these creatures as spells in the hope that the real animal would then be pleased or controlled. Dedi's wax crocodile is a reflection of this.

Hermes Trismegistus was a neo-Platonist take on the messenger of the gods, Hermes, aka Mercury – who himself, of course, was an evolution from the earlier Thoth. (Mary Evans Picture Library)

Mercurius Trismegistus.

Quòd Iove sis genitus magno, vis enthea mentis Divinæ, et cœli cognitio alta probat.

Hermes Thrice-Great

Egypt was flooded, and only a small remnant of humanity remained, clinging to a high mountain. As the waters receded, a traveler approached, leaning on a staff even though wings sprouted from his boots. Two snakes coiled around his staff, and he had shining hair and a strange young-old face.

"Who are you?" a ragged survivor asked. "Where have you come from, and how did you survive the Flood?"

The man smiled kindly and said, "I am Hermes, called Twice-Great, and I have walked from Babylon to heal you, teach you, and lead you home."

The people gathered their belongings and began their journey across an expanse of black mud.

"Don't be afraid," said Hermes. "I will show you everything you need." He threw a handful of seeds into the mud. Green shoots appeared immediately. Then he took a stick, and he drew the shapes of animals, birds, and fish in the mud. He drew houses and strange conical buildings with triangular sides. He drew smiling faces, stars, the sun, the moon, and a face in a crown, upon which a serpent reared.

An apology by the author, Roger Bacon, with a portrait of Hermes Trismegistus, "father of philosophy," in his 1557 *Miroir d'Alchimie*. (Library of Congress)

"Remember these signs," said Hermes. "The gods have given them to you so you can build houses, grow crops, and know when to harvest them. You can measure and build and weigh and compare. You will build houses for your children, temples for your gods, and, when you die, your descendants will build your tombs and put my writings in them, so you can climb up to the regions of the eternal unmoving stars and be with those who created you. The heavens resemble the earth. For that which is above is like that which is below."

As he spoke, a star shot across the sky, and a piece of dark metal fell to earth. When it had cooled, Hermes took it in his hand, then put it in a campfire. "Look in the fire," he said, "and tell me what you see."

"I see a bird with many colored tails," said one voice.

"A strange horned beast breathing fire," said another.

And yet another said, "A pharaoh and his queen embrace on a bed, but a great serpent is hidden there. He approaches, he bites. He has killed the pharaoh!"

"Fear not," said Hermes. "Your pharaoh will rise again, stronger than ever, and all who touch him will be immortal. For I have brought you the secrets of alchemy." He fashioned beautiful jewelry for the people to wear, created paint for their faces and forged weapons. He then brought forth a shining white stone, had them build a Great Pyramid and set the stone on the apex.

Hermes showed them how to measure the time, how the heavens governed their lives, and how they themselves were, and are, a part of the stars that revolve. "As above, so below," he said repeatedly.

When Hermes was 10,000 years old, he called for his son, also called Hermes.

"Bring me a piece of emerald, two cubits long, hewn from one whole stone, and an iron stylus. Write down the secrets that I have taught you. The Emerald Tablet will stay here in my tomb for all eternity. You may copy its words, and take the secrets of magic to the world. For you will be Hermes the Thrice-Great. Be careful whom you take as your apprentice and do not trust too easily. Hide your wisdom in pictures and riddles so that only the true of heart can properly understand it."

Hermes Trismegistus then went forth to find an apprentice and bid him copy the book for himself. In time, that apprentice found himself an apprentice from a land far across the desert, and he in turn found another apprentice who, upon his initiation, took the name Hermes. And thus all true books of magic are copies of this one book.

The Historical Hermes Trismegistus and Hermeticism

Just as Christianity later mapped its saints' days onto existing pagan feast days, so ancient Greece mapped the attributes of its gods onto Egyptian deities such as Thoth, who gave the knowledge of writing and magic to mankind. In the middle of the 2nd century BC, the legend arose of a wizard who had hidden a magical book, written on a single sheet of emerald with an iron pen, in the tomb of his divine namesake.

Nobody is quite sure where the name "Thrice-Great" came from, though it may derive from a reference to Thoth at the Temple of Esna, which describes him as "the Great, the Great, and the Great."

This is an image of Hermes originally inlaid on the floor of Siena Cathedral, but now on the wall (Mary Evans Picture Library / Iberfoto)

By the 5th century AD, theologians and students of magic and myth who had taken the name "Hermeticists" had come to the conclusion that "Hermes Trismegistus" was the author of an influential series of magical texts, named the Emerald Books after the legendary texts inscribed onto actual emerald. They also believed he had prophesied the coming of Christianity and may have taken the name because he was the third of a series of men sharing the pseudonym Hermes, one of whom translated Thoth's writings.

The original Emerald Book never actually existed, but the Trismegistus "translation" has existed in multiple editions in several languages. Hermes's motto, "as above, so below," was used in 15th-century Europe to define the relationships between the earthly and the heavenly, and formed the backbone of western magical and scientific thinking.

ALCHEMY

Alchemy is the science, or art, of changing one type of matter into another. Many important discoveries of early chemistry came out of alchemical experiments to find a way of turning base metals into gold. In fact, the word "chemistry" comes from the Arabic word "al-chemi." The practical premise of alchemy was obviously flawed, although today base metals can be turned into precious ones with the help of a particle collider, but only at the sub-atomic level, and at astronomical cost.

Experiments conducted in pursuit of this dream were elaborate and rigorous, and led to genuine scientific discoveries, such as alloys like brass, used in coinage and in scientific instruments for centuries. The earliest scientists were the alchemist and magus in their laboratories, surrounded by distillation vessels and encoded texts. Sir Isaac Newton, father of modern physics, was an alchemist. So great was the association of alchemy with wizardry that his alchemical notes were hidden for more than 100 years out of fear of what those interests might do to his academic reputation.

The historical role of alchemy has been as a cause of the transmission of knowledge. Many alchemical authors claimed that their works were copies or translations of

Woodcuts illustrating the alchemical processes of distillation and filtration for a 1531 edition of *De Alchimia Libri Tres*, attributed to Geber, under the name "Dshabir ibn Hayyan." (INTERPHOTO / Sammlung Raach / Mary Evans)

much older ones, given to them by strangers. These texts were allegorical, often telling stories in which metals were protagonists who meet, marry, die, and get devoured by monsters, reduced to skeletons in the tomb, then buried and reborn.

Gold was represented by the sun and the figure of a king. The moon was a silver queen. Copper was a beautiful Venus, and lead was an old man, Saturn. As the base metal, he was the one who magically delivered the book to the alchemist. Mercury, the catalyst, was the winged god, a dragon, or a snake swallowing his own tail. The object with the power of transmutation was often depicted as a salamander, which could re-grow a severed limb and was thought to be born from fire, because real salamanders like to sleep in the exact type of wood that is best for firewood and so would often wake up in a fireplace.

SIMON MAGUS'S BATTLE WITH ST PETER (OVERLEAF)

There are many different versions of Simon Magus's battle with future saints, then-apostles, Peter and Paul, in the forum in Rome. Some versions suggest that Peter and Paul stayed on the ground and shot him down with Prayer, others have the demons drawing Simon's chariot turn on him. In one story the confrontation consists simply of a debate around the Emperor Nero's dining table.

Simon Magus

Simon Magus left home with ambitions to make something of himself, to get an education he could not receive in a one-goat town like Gitta, his home village some 30 miles north of Jerusalem. He wanted to see the world and be a part of the wonders of Rome and Jerusalem.

Soon after leaving home, Simon became friends with a mysterious girl named Helen, a girl he felt that he had always known.

"Perhaps in another life," she told him.

Helen understood Simon's lust for knowledge, so she took him to a meeting of students taught by John the Baptist. Fascinated by John's teachings, Simon was baptized by John's friend Philip. He became one of John's best students and closest friends. However, he also made an enemy in a man named Dositheus, who also had an interest in Helen.

John recommended that Simon study at the great Greek schools of literature in Alexandria. There, Simon devoured the tales of the workings of gods, heroes, and kings, but he was most fascinated by the stories of magicians and prophecy. Simon saw aspects of himself in these old stories, and soon committed many spells and rituals to memory. He also recognized Helen as the reincarnation of Helen of Troy, and now understood why they had always known each other. They had both lived before during the Trojan War.

When John the Baptist was beheaded, someone had to take over the group.

"We need to recall Simon," said Helen, but Dositheus disagreed.

"That cannot be," he told them sadly. "A message arrived from Alexandria; Simon is also dead." Nobody had any reason to doubt him, and so Dositheus proclaimed himself to be the "Standing One."

Soon, however, Simon returned. At first, Simon was sanguine, acknowledging Dositheus as the leader. This embarrassed and unnerved Dositheus, who grabbed a strong staff and knocked Simon to his knees. Simon called upon the spells and powers he had learned from the ancient texts. Dositheus raised his staff for a killing blow, but as he brought it down, the weapon passed clean through Simon as it would have gone through a column of smoke.

Dositheus fell to his knees, amazed. "You are truly the Standing One! Then I will follow you." As well as the leadership, Dositheus also lost his chances with Helen, whom Simon wooed with the knowledge that they were both reincarnations of earlier demigods.

Soon, stories spread of how Simon conjured the soul out of a boy in order to have it as his familiar spirit, and how he used his powers to persuade the king's sister to marry the Procurator – the province's Roman treasurer – instead of the man the king had arranged for her to marry.

A Duel in the Sky

It was not long before the fame of Simon spread far and wide, and came to the attention of Peter and John, two of the apostles of Jesus of Nazareth. Worried that Simon was using the power of demons to imitate God, they decided to go to the market square in Jerusalem to hear the magus speak.

When the apostles arrived, Simon was not there, so they began preaching and blessing people in Jesus's name. They healed the sick and brought hope to the downtrodden. As they were teaching, Simon arrived. Impressed by the obvious power of the two apostles, Simon went up to Peter and offered to buy the knowledge behind his power.

Peter shook his head. "This power cannot be bought. Your heart is not right in the sight of God. Repent and pray to God."

"You can pray for me," Simon said and stomped off.

Sometime later, Peter and another apostle, Paul, saw Simon in the forum in Rome. They heard Simon say, "Soon, my friends, I will travel up to heaven to meet with God."

Offended by Simon's audacity, Peter called for him to prove it.

Simon spread his hands, began muttering under his breath, and levitated into the air above the crowd. Peter immediately closed his eyes in prayer, and rose into the air himself, blocking Simon's path. Peter swooped towards him with the power of God blazing through him. Simon's concentration broke, and he fell onto the cobbles with a cracking of bone. Seeing that he was just a man who had tricked them, the crowd rushed forward, hurling stones.

This colored woodcut from the *Nuremberg Liber Chronicarum* of 1492 shows Simon Magus being cut to pieces in the middle of a battle between saints and demons. (The Bridgeman Art Library)

Simon couldn't flee on his shattered leg and quickly incanted another spell. A chariot, drawn by demons, swept down and scooped him up, but before he got far Peter and Paul leapt into action. Their prayers called down the power of God upon the demonic carriage, which immediately disintegrated, pieces falling to earth as the demons scattered. This time, when Simon's body hit the ground, it did not rise.

The Historical Simon of Gitta

Simon Magus was a local religious leader in Samaria who converted to Christianity, but remained involved with a Gnostic sect. He is also said to have taken money for prayers, and this type of bribery became known as Simony. Others have suggested that his sect was involved with the promotion of "free love."

In the apocryphal *Acts of Peter* Simon lands in the Sacra Via, the main road through Rome, and is carried 40 miles to the town of Terracina, to be seen by a surgeon named Castor, who himself has been banished due to an accusation of sorcery. Simon then dies "while being sorely cut by two physicians."

Local myth has it that the church of Santa Francesca Romana was built on the spot where Simon landed, and it contains a marble slab supposedly bearing the imprints of the knees of Peter and Paul. Medieval versions of the story have Simon employed by Nero and suggest that there was a statue of him in Rome. This, however, conflates him with another Simon, who was Jewish rather than Samaritan. These medieval legends were an influence on Christopher Marlowe's version of Faust.

This is an 1890 view of the site of the Roman forum, where Peter and Paul had their showdown with Simon Magus. On the mid-left you can see the 12th-century tower of the Santa Francesca church where Simon supposedly landed. The Colosseum beyond would later host Cellini's unfortunate magical ritual. (Library of Congress)

WIZARDS OF THE
FIRST MILLENNIUM

Virgil

Publius Vergilius Maro, who would come to be better known as the Roman writer and statesman Virgil, was said to be the son of a magus named Stimicho and Magia Polla, which meant "she who is great." Jupiter sprinkled golden flakes into Magia's wine to ensure that the couple conceived a powerful son. While pregnant, Magia had visions of giving birth to a laurel twig, which grew into a tree covered in flowers and fruit, while music played and the gods rejoiced. A poet said this meant that their son would be a famous poet, and that they should name him Vergilius, after the Latin name for the laurel tree. When Virgil was born he already had teeth and was able to walk immediately.

A 15th-century portrait (1475) of Virgil by the Flemish painter Joost Van Gent, which is now in the Louvre. (The Bridgeman Art Library)

The family kept secret the fact that he had been born with teeth, lest fearful villagers try to kill him.

When Virgil was seven, he ran to his uncle's field. "Will you help me in the battle, Uncle?" he asked. "A black bull is coming, and you must strike it and keep striking it."

"Of course," his uncle said, not willing to leave his nephew undefended.

"If I win," Virgil said, "our land will always be prosperous, but I will go away for seven years. No one must ever know where I've gone. You must tell no one what has happened."

Soon, a massive storm rolled across the field, and a gigantic black bull appeared on the horizon. It charged towards Virgil, but his uncle interceded, hitting it with his staff. As his uncle continued to hit the bull, however, Virgil himself changed, in a flash of lightning, into a giant white bull. As the two massive animals locked horns, their hooves churning the earth, more

19

storm clouds descended, tearing them from the ground. Both bulls, locked in combat, sprouted wings as they struggled. The thunder faded, and Virgil's uncle was left alone and troubled in his field.

The Mantuan Seer

Virgil returned after seven years and went to an ancient ruined temple to sleep. Soon he heard an unearthly voice, claiming to be an imprisoned demon, trapped in an urn under a stone. When Virgil broke it open, a beautiful woman emerged, and gave him a book of spells and a magic wand as his reward for freeing her.

Virgil was now at the age of maturity and was declared a magus as well as a man. He took on students to learn magic from him, and they called him the Mantuan Seer. One of his students was the nephew of the emperor, and, through him, Virgil once asked the emperor "Which is more useful to you: a bird that kills other birds, or a fly that catches other flies?"

"The fly," the emperor said immediately. "In Naples there are so many flies they make the walls black, and they ruin all the food."

Demons swarm around Dante and his guide, Virgil, in this 19th-century Gustave Doré illustration for *The Divine Comedy*. (PD)

"A wise choice," Virgil agreed, and he returned to his villa, where he began to sculpt a golden fly the size of a frog. He combined notes from many alchemical and astrological texts into a spell, cast it upon the golden fly, and then installed it on a column by the city gate. The fly drew other flies to it, where they died, and the city's food suddenly improved.

Ever more students came to learn from Virgil, and he taught them proverbs that were secret spells for summoning feminine spirits of wisdom called Gnomai. He also taught spells to the Gnomai themselves, and called his spells "Gnomes." One student was Gaius Pollio, who would later be a governor of part of Gaul. Virgil taught Pollio the Gnome: "*Ne respondeas tu sine, certe auscultato fine,*" which means "You should not answer, until you are sure you've heard all to the end."

One day Pollio discovered a stone with the word "lift" carved upon it. Underneath was a gold ring, engraved with sigils. He put on the ring and went to sleep in a nearby granary. Soon two brothers came in furtively.

"I'm glad our father told us about the ring he hid under the stone before he died. But if only he'd told us where the stone was!"

Pollio thought to hand over the ring, but remembered Virgil's teaching. He hesitated, and the brothers continued. "I'll use the ring to turn my teacher into an ass," the first said, "and beat him for punishing me for being drunk."

The other brother nodded, and said, "I'll change the count's daughter into a bitch in heat."

Pollio knew he was right to obey the Gnome and keep quiet. He put a note under the stone, saying the spirits had taken custody of the ring so that the evil brothers couldn't abuse its power.

The Gallic Slave

Virgil was also known for his skill in necromancy, the art of calling upon the spirits of the dead. For this art, he ritually confined his diet to dairy produce and eggs. He would walk as a wandering scholar and beg for milk from houses. As a wizard, he already knew who had milk to spare, and when someone refused to share it, Virgil would open his black book and cast a hailstorm upon the house.

One household always sent an educated Gallic slave to bring Virgil milk, and Virgil enjoyed chatting with him. Virgil decided to reward the household for their generosity, which showed great honor to Jupiter.

"Tell your master that he should dig in this place I have drawn. Three cubits deep in the earth there is a chest of money, but also tell him not to plan what to do with this money before he has finished digging. If he does, he will die."

The slave told this to his master, who took his brother and the slave to the location Virgil had indicated. There they had the slave dig and found a solid oaken chest.

When they got the chest to the lip of the hole, the master nudged his brother and said, "We'll split this between us, fifty-fifty. The slave has no need of it." Instantly, the ground crumbled, and the brothers collapsed. The chest

This illustration for the Gustav Doré version of *The Divine Comedy* reflects Virgil's reputation of being a necromancer in its depiction of a decapitated spirit holding up its head in one hand. (PD)

slid back on top of the slave, pushing him towards the bottom of the hole. Instead of crushing him, however, it pushed him into a tunnel. Slave and chest tumbled to a halt in a small room.

The slave felt around in the dark, his hands pushing a small door, behind which Virgil and his students were waiting for the slave. Virgil had been suspicious of the master's likely actions. He gave the slave the contents of the chest and invited him to join their group, so that his education could continue. The slave went on to become a powerful necromancer.

The Last Spells

Naples fell under a curse, which required the city walls to be reconsecrated, as Romulus and Remus had consecrated the walls of Rome. Virgil knew that the spell required the egg of a gryphon, and since no such thing existed any longer, he would create one.

A line was drawn around an ostrich egg, one half coated in bronze and fitted with a gold sun, the other half in dark blue paint and fitted with a silver moon. It was then sealed in a glass ampoule, and Virgil incanted a verse from Aristophanes' *The Birds* while walking clockwise around the city. The egg was then fumigated in sulphur vapor. It was placed in a cage, atop four columns, on a bronze pillar, in a castle to be guarded forever, the Castel Marino.

"If ever the egg is broken," Virgil warned, "Naples will fall into the sea."

Virgil knew when and where he would die, and so had prepared his own tomb. First he opened a cave by the sheer force of his gaze, inside of which was built a small temple, where white marble columns would support the vessel containing his bones.

VIRGIL AS THE GUIDE THROUGH THE INFERNO.

Dante Alighieri didn't just pick Virgil out of the air to be his guide through the underworld in *The Divine Comedy*. The Roman writer had been considered a wizard throughout the medieval era, and he was not alone; Faust and other figures thought to be wizards are among the denizens of the underworld, as a medieval Christian would expect of those who consorted with demons. Virgil, however, got special status as narrator, as he was thought, after the 4th century, to have prophesied the coming and righteousness of Christianity.

Sure enough, when the Emperor Augustus came to bring him to Rome in September of 19 BC, Virgil knew his time had come, and he settled all his affairs. He died on the road near Brindisi on September 20.

The Historical Virgil

Virgil was born to an equestrian family near Mantua in October of 70 BC, and is probably best known for the *Aeneid*, the epic tale of the founding of Rome. He was educated in Cremona, Milan, and Rome, and originally trained to be a lawyer before he took to poetry. His *Aeneid* was his last work, and he was unsatisfied with it, so, when he fell ill with a fever in September of 19 BC, he left instructions that it be burned upon his death. The Emperor Augustus, however, was a big fan, and overruled this wish, forcing his executors to publish it instead.

Because the *Aeneid* was seen as the central cultural epic about the Latinized peoples of Europe, it was a vital part of church-approved literature in Christian antiquity, though Virgil himself pre-dated Christianity. The fourth book of his *Eclogues* was said to prophesize the coming of Christ. This legitimized him in the Christian world, and making him a prophet led to other powers being attributed to him.

By the Middle Ages, Virgil was popularly cast as a powerful wizard in folk tales and fairytales, and Dante Alighieri casts him as the narrator's guide to purgatory in *The Divine Comedy*. Many of these tales were adapted from other myths and folklore, even to the extent that his birth was adapted from the story of Zeus turning into a shower of gold before Danaë. In one version of the story of the demon who gave Virgil his black book, the demon trapped Virgil in the hole from which it had emerged, which is a common theme with stories about genies.

In fact, so prevalent was the view of Virgil as a magician that there was a medieval fashion for attempting divination from his writings, seeking hidden knowledge within them.

Jabir ibn Hayyan in a 15th-century Florentine illustration. (© Photo Researchers / Mary Evans Picture Library)

Abu Musa Jabir Ibn Hayyan, aka Geber

The caliph marched into Jabir's laboratory, eyes wide in his white-bearded face, while the midnight blue robes of the vizier Ja'far emerged from the shadows beside him.

The chubby caliph leaned forward excitedly, stroking his white whiskers. "Why did you want to see me? Have you a new toy?"

"Perhaps, Excellency," Jabir said with a smile. "I have been thinking about the need for increasing the numbers of our soldiers."

"You plan to open a recruiting office?" Ja'far asked dryly.

"Not at all," the alchemist said. "Have you read my *Book of Stones*?"

"Of course," Ja'far nodded. "It was very precise, as a book of the sciences should be."

"It was ... confusing," said the caliph.

"In it, I discussed Takwin, the creation of different forms of life. I believe that those processes can be extended to man, and that would be an obvious solution to keeping up the numbers of our guards and soldiers."

Jabir led the pair to the main table in the room. "Observe." He indicated a particularly complex set up of distillation equipment, cauldrons of burning powder, and a copper bowl at the far end of the arrangement. "The essential salts are mixed according to the principles of Aristotelian elements."

Jabir had his visitors peer into the bowl. Droplets of metallic liquid trickled

MAGIC WORDS – ANCIENT AND MODERN

It's not just what you say, it's how you say it. Greco-Roman wizards thought that the most important ingredient in a spell was actually sung not spoken, and included strings of onomatopoeic vowels such as AAAAEEEIIIIOOOUUU in their magical instructions.

The most famous magic word, "Abracadabra," is actually Aramaic, taken from the words "A'bra," meaning "I create," "ca," meaning "what," and "dabra," meaning "I speak." The phrase "I create what I speak" thus harks back to some very old beliefs about a thing and the word that it describes being identical.

Popular languages for use in magic in the Middle Ages included Latin, Hebrew, Greek, and Arabic, but many wizards also invented their own tongues and scripts. Dr John Dee and Edward Kelley, for example, wrote in Enochian, "the language of the angels," which was itself a medieval invention.

Successful wizards needed to be multilingual, as the magical text the *Key of Solomon* shows. A wizard might, for example, want to summon the spirits Azazel (a prince of Hell, named in Arabic), Michael, Uriel, Gabriel (Hebrew names for archangels) Bellerophon (Greek), or whatever. It was always, of course, important to get your magical words right, as Harry Potter demonstrates when he attempts to reach Diagon Alley, misspeaks the spell as "diagonally," and ends up in trouble.

It could be that any words work as "magic words" so long as they are suitably impressive and the people saying them believe in and focus on them. This is amply illustrated by the Master in the Dr. Who story *The Daemons* (1971) where, after calling out "Io evohe" (a Romanization of the Greek equivalent of the tetragrammaton, the vowels, EUOI, and, in context, pretty much meaning "pay attention!"), he chants "mallett tiladah yram," which is just "Mary had a little lam[b]" backwards.

slowly in, combining, assembling, and growing glistening segmented legs and tails. Soon, a number of scorpions were clattering around in the bowl.

The caliph drew back with a grimace, as Ja'far leaned in to cast an impressed eye over them. "Neatly done."

"I have made scorpions and snakes. The principle would also apply to men, but I would require larger equipment and greater resources …"

"Ah, you're asking for money," the caliph said. "Well, the best toys are expensive, I suppose."

"And sometimes our enemies' coffers are deep," Ja'far said darkly. "What is to stop them buying you from us?"

Jabir laughed. "I do what I do because Allah loves me for it, not for gold."

"Next you'll be telling me gold is worthless to you," the caliph snorted.

"What if I proved that it was?" Jabir held out a hand. "Do you have a gold object you're willing never to see again? A coin, a tooth, a ring?"

Ja'far flipped him a coin, which Ibn Hayyan caught neatly. "Show me."

Jabir moved to a desk which held a dish of salts and two jars. He mixed the three together in one glass jar, and a foul vapor emerged. "Watch." He dropped the coin into the water. Immediately, the coin began to bubble and fade as it sank. In a moment, it was gone. Ja'far and the caliph exchanged a glance.

There is more than one person given the Geber name. This is a 14th-century illustration of a "Spanish alchemist Geber" teaching in Greece, though the one definitely-known Spanish "Geber" is Jabir ibn Aflah, who was an astronomer and mathematician who invented the torquetum. (Mary Evans Picture Library)

The older man said, "What about equipment and servants?"

"I would be most grateful," Jabir said. And he continued to be so, and continued to serve the caliph for many more years.

The Three Historical Gebers

"Geber" was originally a Romanization of the name of the 8th-century Arab astrologer, physician, and philosopher Abu Musa Jabir ibn Hayyan, who became an alchemist at the court of Caliph Haroun al Rashid, and who was a physician for the vizier Ja'far ibn Yahya.

Ibn Hayyan's research pioneered the modern scientific method of insisting upon repeatable experimentation, so that a result of an experiment could only be relied upon if it could be repeated. He developed the processes of calcination, distillation, sublimation, and evaporation. He also discovered nitric, hydrochloric, acetic, and citric acids. He is also credited with inventing many items of chemical equipment, including the alembic and the retort.

The frontispiece for Oswald Kroll's *Basilica Chymica*, depicting six founding fathers of Alchemy, with Ibn Hayyan at the top left. Kroll was another of Rudolf II's pet alchemists and knew Edward Kelley. He was heavily involved with both alchemy and chemistry, and influential in treating the two as separate sciences. (INTERFOTO / Alamy)

He was a prolific author, publishing nearly 200 works, including the *Book of Venus*, *On the Noble Art of Alchemy*, and the *Book of Stones* (which includes his recipes for creating snakes and scorpions) all of which are a part of a set called *The Seventy Books*. He also translated Hermes Trismegistus's Emerald Tablet as part of *The Hundred and Twelve Books*, and wrote *The Ten Books of Rectification*, which are about the lives and works of Greek philosophers.

These books were published in Europe under the name Geber, which became a sort of brand name. As a result, there is still uncertainty in academia over whether Ibn Hayyan was the original Geber, or even existed at all. What is known for certain is that there is a corpus of works originally in Arabic that details these discoveries, but there are also various works under the name Geber that only exist in Latin and had no Arabic original.

The term "gibberish" for an incomprehensible technical language derives from the name Geber, due to the complexity of his – or their – works.

THE WIZARD OF CAMELOT

Merlin

The king of Demetia had rich lands, a queen, and four children, but had got on the wrong side of the Devil, who set out for revenge. First the Devil sent a pestilence so that the crops failed, and all the livestock in Demetia died. Next, a demon killed the king's only son in his bed, and the grief was so great that the queen hanged herself. The king himself died of a broken heart.

There were still the king's three daughters to deal with. One was shown to be an adulteress and executed, and the second was lured by a witch into becoming a prostitute and selling her soul. The last princess sought the help of a priest called Blaise, who advised her to avoid temptation and anger, and enabled her to become a nun so that she would be protected. Her older sister, however, was able to visit her in the nunnery, making her angry. The sin of wrath, therefore, allowed the Devil to attack the younger princess from within. An incubus came to her in her dreams and seduced her, thus fathering a child upon her.

Luckily, Blaise suspected that an incubus was responsible, as the princess had slept alone in a locked room. She would not be executed for adultery, at least not before her baby had been born. Two women were sent to help her give birth, but both were horrified when out popped a baby boy covered in coarse black fur. Blaise made sure that the princess sent her baby to be baptized, and she named him after her late father, the king: Merlin.

When Merlin was 18 months old, and the local judges were determined to execute the princess for adultery, Merlin said he would save her. When she was brought before the judge for sentencing, he spoke up.

"I will prove my mother's innocence, and the guilt of others," he promised. "I know everyone's father," the toddler said to the head judge, "including yours."

"If you prove her innocence," the head judge said, "I will spare the princess. If not, you'll burn with her."

"Let me tell you of your own father," Merlin said. "Your mother said he died when you were a baby. But he lives and gives sermons every Sunday." Merlin pointed to a local priest.

The judge's mother, who was watching her son at work, paled.

"This boy is the Devil," she said. "The Prince of Lies!"

"So you deny you still lie with him?" Merlin asked. "That he shared your bed last night?"

The judge's mother broke down then and confessed that all this was true. Since the judge would have had to send his own mother to burn if he condemned the princess, he cleared her.

Merlin then told the court that his true father was an incubus, and that he could see both the past, owing to his demonic heritage, and the future, because of the godly influence of his baptism, which combated it. He predicted that the judge's true father would drown himself, and this proved to be true also. The judges of the kingdom then proclaimed Merlin a wise man, though he was only 18 months old.

Blaise remained a friend of Merlin, and some say that it was he who first chronicled the story of Arthur and the Grail, and Merlin's part in that great adventure.

Vortigern and the Dragons

The king of the Britons, Vortigern, wanted to build a stone tower as his keep, but the

Gustave Doré gives us a seminal wizard image – long beard, robes, wand, etc – in this study of Merlin tutoring young Arthur. (PD)

tower would always crumble and fall when it was half done. His advisers suggested that he must have a protective spell cast, by mixing the cement for the foundations with the blood of a fatherless child.

Merlin was brought to him, now an adolescent. When he was told that he was to be sacrificed, Merlin scoffed at the king's advisers.

"That is the most ridiculous thing I've ever heard," he told them to their faces. "I have a vision of what lies beneath your foundations. A deep pool, upon which no stone can stand. Within the pool sleep two dragons, one red and one white. When they awake, they find themselves still trapped, and fight out of frustration. This is what shakes the walls of your tower to rubble."

Vortigern immediately ordered his workmen to dig underneath the site for the tower. They eventually struck water, and, with a tremendous storm of spray and roaring of fire, the two dragons burst forth, clawing and flaming at each other as they ascended, still locked in combat.

"The red dragon stands for the Britons," Merlin warned, "the white for the Saxons. The boar of Cornwall, who shall be king of the Britons, will drive the Saxons out, but after six generations, they will return to fight again." The foundation of Vortigern's tower was now stable, and the masons could finish its construction.

Stonehenge

After Vortigern, Merlin became a strategic adviser to his successor, Aurelius Ambrosius. As Merlin was able to see all the events of the past, he had the knowledge of all the great generals of history, such as Alexander the Great, and so his advice was well-chosen, and the British armies found themselves becoming ever more victorious against the Saxons.

Ambrosius saw his chance to wipe out the Saxon invaders for good after a huge battle that left 3,000 of his own knights dead on Salisbury Plain. As the invaders were surrounded, Merlin brought his horse beside the king's, and said, "A word, my liege. Do not take any further action. The temptation to slay unarmed men is not Christian."

Morality was only part of his reason, of course. He knew the future, and could not allow the king to alter it. Reluctantly, Ambrosius allowed the defeated Saxons to escape, leaving only the dead.

"We should build a memorial here to our dead. One that will last forever."

Ambrosius tasked Merlin with acquiring rocks with magical properties for the memorial. These rocks were known as the Giants' Dance, because giants had brought them from Africa. The problem was that the Giants' Dance was currently on Mount Killaraus in Ireland, and the Irish were not keen on giving the stones up. Ambrosius, therefore, gave Merlin 15,000 knights, led by his own brother, Uther, as back-up.

The Irish fielded a huge army to defend against this invasion, but were simply outclassed. Uther's knights smashed into them, killing 7,000, and securing Mount Killaraus. The Britons then set about trying to dismantle the

Stonehenge remains standing, even in the present. (Author's collection)

STONEHENGE

Merlin is associated with Stonehenge because of the pervasiveness of the Arthurian cycle and the traditional – if erroneous – association of the place with the druids, as Merlin has been seen as the most famous druid.

Our view of the druids is largely fictitious, based on medieval and later nationalist interpretations of a short passage in the writings of the Roman historian Tacitus, and the creative scholarship of figures like Inigo Jones and John Aubrey. These interpretations attributed all pre-historical building to white-robed, sickle-wielding figures who inhabited a mythical age of human sacrifice in oak groves and giant wicker men, in between magically repelling Roman invasion fleets.

There is an obvious association with Wales, as the bluestones at Stonehenge are known to come from Preselli, and Merlin is often a Welsh figure. There is also a tradition that the area of Amesbury in Wiltshire is named for Ambrosius, and that he ordered Stonehenge built.

In reality the site was probably constructed by a Neolithic agrarian community *c.* 2500 BC – long before the Romans – as a solar calendar. Most recent research suggests it was part of a much larger landscape involving nearby Woodhenge and numerous barrows and was constantly redeveloped over several centuries.

Giants' Dance for transport. They threw ropes around the stones, hundreds of men hauling on each rope, but the stones stayed right where they were.

Frustrated, Uther went to Merlin, who said, "As I expected. Prepare for the journey home, while I take care of the Giants' Dance."

The knights didn't believe that one man could do what hundreds couldn't, but knew better than to disobey their leader. Merlin, meanwhile, jammed the end of his staff under the base of a stone and pressed down on the other end. The stone popped out of its setting easily, and Merlin moved to the next one and repeated the feat. When Uther and his men set sail, they were astonished to see all the stones floating along beside them.

Ambrosius and his entourage on Salisbury Plain were surprised to see Merlin guiding the stones into a great circle. Under Merlin's direction, the great stones whispered smoothly through the air like dancers, while the huge lintel slabs settled on them as softly as a butterfly's landing. In hours, the great circular monument of Stonehenge was complete.

The Woodsman

In Brittany, Merlin encountered a poor woodsman, whose family was starving because the local mayor had imposed punitive taxes on his population in order to distribute money among his friends.

"Can you help me?" he asked Merlin.

Merlin told the woodsman to cut down a certain tree, and he would find a treasure. "Use the treasure wisely," Merlin warned him.

The woodsman promised that he would, and he meant it. He went to the tree and found the treasure, an old hoard from before the Romans. The woodsman invested the treasure wisely, renovating his house and making sure

his family was better fed. He then made friends and promised to reduce the taxes if he was made mayor. Soon he was.

At first he kept his promise and reduced the taxes and rents. However, his new rich friends had infectious tastes, and before long he was as selfish and greedy as the previous mayor.

One morning, he met another woodsman, with shaggy hair and oversized boots and clothes. "I need your help, sir," this woodsman said. "I have no food left after the taxes. Do you have some you could spare?"

"Certainly not," the now-mayor replied. "There are plenty of rabbits in the forest, aren't there?"

"And plenty of sad tales too," the woodsman replied. Suddenly, he was Merlin, in his finest robes. "Such as a man who has forgotten his promises."

With that, Merlin put a curse on him that he should lose all that he had gained, and more. Within a month, his wife had taken a lover from among his friends, the crops had failed, reducing tax income, and he was losing money hand over fist. When he was a poor woodsman again, he regretted ever having met Merlin.

The Carnac Stones

Such activities had brought Merlin to the attention of the ruling Romans, who sought to take him to Rome as a prize. Near the Breton village of Carnac, a legion surrounded him, ordering him to submit and come along quietly.

"I am no plaything for your emperor," he warned them. "I will see him in due time, but I am not at your beck and call."

"When the emperor commands," the centurion in charge said, "the world obeys."

As one, the well-drilled Romans took up their traditional square formation, and marched on Merlin. Looking forward to a reward from the emperor, the centurion led the advance himself, wanting to be the first to clap Merlin in irons.

Merlin shook his head and plunged the end of his staff into the earth. Immediately, a wave of light burst forth, spreading across the field, and where it touched a Roman soldier that man was turned instantly to stone. When the light faded, all that remained was Merlin, standing before a series of rows of stones, which still stand at Carnac today.

The Roman Emperor

Merlin then heard that the emperor, Julius Caesar, was suffering from bad dreams. He changed himself into a white stag, and presented himself before Caesar in Rome. At first Caesar thought there would be fine venison that night, but the stag spoke.

"An emperor who has bad dreams might not be hungry."

"What do you mean?" Caesar demanded. "What do you know of my dreams?"

"They keep you awake, and sicken your stomach. You ponder their meaning in every waking moment, but there is one who can reveal their meaning."

"Who is it? Is it you?"

"Not I, but the wild man of the woods. Find him, and he will reveal the secrets of the dream."

With that, the stag leapt over the heads of the people in the forum, and ran out of the city. Caesar announced a reward for anyone who could bring the wild man to him. Merlin, meanwhile, went to the daughter of a German noble who had been in trouble with Caesar over a claim of adultery. As the stag, he led her into the woods and disappeared.

Soon, she stumbled across a wild man, covered in rags.

"Do you know about dreams?" she asked.

MERLIN DIRECTING THE GIANTS' DANCE (OVERLEAF)

Placing Merlin in a particular era is well-nigh impossible, but a Roman or Romano-British setting is a good fit for him. That said, Stonehenge as we recognize it was actually built around 1,500 years before the Romans invaded, on a site that had been used ceremonially for a couple of thousand years before that.

"I may do. Do you have bad dreams?"

The wild man – who was, of course, Merlin – leaned forward.

"The emperor does. There is a reward for finding the one who can tell him what his dreams mean."

"Then you must be a rich girl, for I can do that," said Merlin.

The daughter led him back before Caesar. The emperor gave her the reward money, restoring her family, and then turned to the wild man.

"What do my dreams mean?"

"They are visions," Merlin said. "They mean that someone close to you is surrounded by a falseness intended to confuse you. There are 12 hidden people who thwart you and you do not know it."

The only group of 12 people that Caesar knew was his wife's handmaidens. When he brought them to the forum, the wild man suddenly lunged, tearing the clothes from them, revealing to a shocked crowd that they were men - lovers that the empress had disguised. Merlin then revealed himself and gave the emperor a lecture on the sins of greed and lustfulness.

The Birth of Arthur

In time, a comet appeared in the sky in the shape of a dragon. Merlin knew this portent meant that Ambrosius was dead. Merlin crowned Uther "Pendragon" after the comet that had brought him to the throne.

Soon afterwards, Uther fell for Ygraine, the wife of Gorloise of Cornwall, whose symbol was a boar. Uther asked Merlin to cast a glamour that would make him look like Gorloise. Reluctantly, Merlin agreed, knowing that it was necessary to fulfill a prophecy he had made earlier. He made Uther promise that any child borne by Ygraine should be handed over to him to do with as he saw fit.

Ygraine, of course, did bear a son, Arthur, who was given into Merlin's care. Merlin, in turn, secretly persuaded the knight, Sir Ector, to adopt the boy. He then told the various barons and local kings around Britain that the true king who would rule them all would be the one man who could draw the sword from the anvil in the stone, which was already legendary.

When Arthur grew up and drew the sword from the stone, Merlin was his adviser. First, however, he used the same power and magic that had built Stonehenge to build Arthur a castle, Camelot. Inside, Merlin also constructed the legendary Round Table, to a design he had received from Joseph of Arimathea.

He predicted that Arthur would face strife with King Pellinore of the Isles, who perpetually hunted the Questing Beast, and whose sons would be fine additions to the Round Table. When Arthur encountered Pellinore during the latter's hunt, they jousted and fought, and the sword in the stone broke upon Pellinore's armor. Merlin brought Arthur and the sword to a lake. There, he tossed the pieces of the sword into the lake, and, in return, Arthur was given the sword Excalibur by the Lady of the Lake.

(Opposite)
Merlin takes the young Arthur to the Lady of the Lake to receive excalibur. Artwork by Alan Lathwell.

"The scabbard's worth ten of the sword," Merlin told the king, "for while you wear it, you cannot bleed from any wound."

Merlin then gave Arthur several prophecies, firstly about the value of the knights Tristan and Lancelot, but also of the treason his queen and his favorite knight would commit between them. He also predicted that, in time, the king would fall ill, and, since the land and the king were one, only the Holy Grail would be able to save them both, and that only the truest of his knights would recover the Grail.

Merlin's Prison

When Arthur visited the king of Northumberland, Merlin was smitten by the Northumbrian king's daughter, Nimue. Nimue, however, did not feel the same way about the aged sorcerer. She knew of some of the tricks he had performed over the years, such as changing Uther into Gorloise, and knew of his demonic heritage. Like many people she was still suspicious of him, despite all he had done for Britain. She told him in no uncertain terms that she could never love him, unless he taught her all he knew of magic.

At first Merlin was reluctant to do so, not least because his powers

This rather touching photo of "Merlin and Vivian" was posed for an edition of Tennyson's *Idylls Of The King* in 1870. The name of the femme fatale in Merlin's story varies according to the telling – Nimue, Vivian, Vivianne, Ninianne, and sometimes she's the Lady of The Lake – but the outcome is always the same. (Library of Congress)

derived from his nature, and could not be replicated by a mortal. Nevertheless, when she and her father visited Camelot later, to stay with Guinevere, Merlin's ardor rekindled, and he relented.

As time passed, Merlin taught Nimue what he knew. She proclaimed that she simply wanted to be sure he could not take advantage of her, but, in truth, she was secretly using his spells to influence his mind and bring him more under her control.

After a few months, Nimue was to return to Northumberland, and Merlin traveled with her. En route, Merlin was troubled by a vision of Mordred, the king's nephew, plotting against Arthur.

"Is something troubling you?" Nimue asked, as they rode through pleasant countryside.

"A vision," Merlin admitted. "Business of the king, not of ours."

"I see." Unbeknownst to Merlin, Nimue really did see, for she had shared his vision, and now saw an opportunity. "Perhaps we should return to Camelot, to help?"

"Yes. It's too dark to ride further now, but I know a place where we can stay the night and go to Camelot at dawn." Merlin led the way to a cave filled with stone columns and ancient statues.

"This place," Nimue asked, "is it your home?"

"One of them, perhaps," Merlin said evasively. "It has been a home to many over the years. A pair of lovers once lived here. When they died, they were placed into one of these stones, to spend eternity together."

"That sounds wonderful," Nimue said. "Wonderful and appropriate."

That night, while Merlin slept, Nimue unlocked the stone that entombed the dead lovers, and found they had long since turned to dust. Then she cast a spell over Merlin so that he couldn't move even if he woke, and put him in the stone before sealing it once more.

When Merlin woke, he found that he was trapped, as the stone could not be opened from the inside, even by his power. Whether Merlin died in the stone tomb or still remains there, driven mad, no one is certain, but he never escaped.

The Two Historical Merlins

Merlin as we think of him today is largely a product of the Sir Thomas Malory's 15th-century *Morte d'Arthur*, a development from Geoffrey of Monmouth's 12th-century *History of the Kings of Britain*, with input from French sources such as the *Livre d'Artus*. Before those legends came along, however, there were already two competing Merlins.

In the 6th century, the king of Demetia, Gwenddoleu, was served and advised by a bard called Myrddin. This Myrddin was a poet and a wise man, but not yet a seer. His king asked him to devise a strategy for a battle against the Scots, soon to take place at Arferydd.

Myrddin studied his maps long into the night and sought guidance in the stars before devising his strategy. When he brought his plan to the king, Gwenddoleu approved it, and the army took up the positions that Myrddin had suggested. When the Scots, led by Ridarch Hael of Strathclyde, took the field, battle was joined. Myrddin was so confident of victory that he took his place in the army, and had encouraged his friends to do so too, so that they could share his and the king's glory.

It was a disaster. Gwenddoleu was killed, as was every man that Myrddin knew. Covered in the blood of his king and his friends, Myrddin fled into the great Caledonian Forest, tearing the gore-covered armor from himself and hurling it away. There he lived alone for many years, driven mad by the horrors he had seen. His broken mind was, however, open to perceiving the future as well as the present, and he was soon scribbling down prophecy after prophecy, surrounded by the forest creatures who were comfortable with him being as wild as they were.

When a saint came to visit Myrddin and receive his confession, Myrddin said that he had been sentenced by God to spend his life as a beast of the forest as penance for getting his king and his friends killed. He then predicted that he himself would die three times: by falling, by stabbing, and by drowning.

Some time later, some of the wild animals that had been around him began harassing the sheep of local farmers. The shepherds knew that the mad wizard lived in the woods and believed that Myrddin must have sent the beasts to cause trouble deliberately. Forming a posse, they hunted Myrddin down, pursuing him along the cliff tops at the coast. As he ran, the cliff edge gave way beneath Myrddin's pounding feet, and he plummeted down onto a piece of wood at the foot of the cliff. Impaled by the wood, Myrddin couldn't move as the tide came in, and he drowned, fulfillling his prophecy.

Other say that Aurelius Ambrosius was himself Merlin, called in Welsh Myrddin Emrys. He was the orphan of Roman parents murdered in a revolt, and King Vortigern ruled only by his permission. In fact, it was said that Vortigern was more afraid of Myrddin Emrys than of any enemy. When Myrddin Emrys revealed the two dragons beneath his tower and predicted the future of Britain, Vortigern named the tower after him: Dinas Emrys, Fort of Ambrosius.

Merlin is, in many ways, the omni-wizard. It is impossible to create a definitive Merlin timeline because the original sources are so diverse. Traditions from Wales, England, Scotland, and France not only feed off each other but also attach the increasingly famous wizard's name to regional stories originally about local characters. The stories also contradict each other, with Ambrosius sometimes being Merlin but more often being a basis for Arthur himself.

Sometimes Merlin is a Scot, sometimes Welsh; sometimes he is ancient by the time of Uther, and sometimes he is Uther's brother. He even manages to visit Julius Caesar (who wasn't actually an emperor, despite the legend calling him so) in Rome sometime in the 40s BC, when he himself is a descendant of 6th-century post-Romans.

Merlin's fame and popularity has never waned. He has always been a solid supporting character in novels and films, whether he is treated as a wise and trustworthy teacher, such as in *The Sword in The Stone*, as a more ambiguous and dangerous figure like Nicol Williamson's version in the movie *Excalibur*, or even as a young man at Uther's court – and boyhood friend of Arthur – in the BBC television series *Merlin*, which ran from 2008 - 2012.

WIZARDS OF THE EAST

Zhang Guo Lao

Zhang Guo was born in Zhongtiao Shan, in Hengzhou Province in central China. His family were farmers, scraping at the soil to make ends meet. As a young man, Zhang Guo would take his family's meager produce to market on the back of his donkey. His route between the farm and the market passed by a long-abandoned monastery, and Zhang Guo would often rest there. One day, he awoke from a doze in the monastery to the smell of cooking. Drawn by the scent, he found a little cauldron over a fire. Bubbling inside was the nicest stew he had ever smelled.

Since the cauldron was in an empty temple, he assumed it was a gift from the gods and shared the stew with his donkey, which had always done the heavy carrying. To his horror, his donkey collapsed, and then his own stomach clenched in agony. Wondering if the gods were punishing him, or if he had been poisoned, he blacked out.

When he awoke, a man was glaring down at him in anger.

"What happened?" asked Zhang Guo.

"You stole my dinner," said the man, "and then you died. And now I'm so angry I would kill you again, if you weren't immortal."

Zhang Guo sat up and saw his donkey was also getting to its feet.

"What are you talking about?" he asked.

"In that cauldron was a potion that I have spent years gathering ingredients to make. It is an ancient recipe that frees the person who consumes it from mortality. So when you ate it, you died to become free from mortality."

"Oh," said Zhang Guo, not really understanding. "What now?"

"Now," the alchemist said, "I'm going to spend the next twenty years trying again. You'll have to sort out your own problems yourself."

The Old Immortal

Years passed. All of Zhang Guo's family died, but he continued to live. With all of time to study, Zhang Guo learned about alchemy and necromancy. He also learned all he could about the arts of winemaking, because he enjoyed wine, and it kept him in touch with his roots.

One day, the great Immortals came to Zhang Guo and tasked him with chasing down a unicorn that was running wild through their lands, the mystical domain which lay somewhere between Heaven and Earth. With his donkey, Zhang Guo pursued the unicorn through these lands and then on through the whole cosmos.

However, because time worked differently there than on Earth, he was vastly aged by the time he returned. Though immortal, he would forever seem to be an old man. Even his donkey's coat had turned white. He was now known as Zhang Guo Lao, meaning "the Elder Zhang Guo."

An Imperial Summons

Zhang Guo Lao was still the helpful – if less hard-working – farmer that he had always been. He traveled around the empire, helping the poor and educating those who wished to become more spiritual. Inevitably, all these good works brought him to the attention of the emperor, who wanted an immortal magician in his government. He dispatched an ambassador to Zhongtiao Shan. After several weeks, the ambassador reached the elder sage.

"I wish to speak with the wise and revered Zhang Guo Lao," he said.

"I am he. What aid do you seek?"

"The emperor has sent me, venerable one, to summon you to the palace, to take an honored place at …"

Before he could finish his message, Zhang Guo Lao toppled over, as stiff as a board. The shocked ambassador found that the man's skin was already cold to the touch. In minutes, Zhang Guo Lao's flesh began to shrivel and drop away from his maggot-covered bones, as if centuries of decay were happening all at once.

Repulsed, the ambassador ordered a couple of his guards to stay the night, in order to bury the body in the morning. However, when the sun dawned the next day, the body was gone.

The Expectant Mother

A thousand miles away, a young man was nervously awaiting the birth of his first child, but his wife, the mother-to-be, was running a fever. Pacing outside his house, the young man spotted a small dust cloud on the horizon. As he watched, an old man came riding towards their house, sitting backwards on a donkey.

"Something troubles this house?" asked Zhang Guo Lao as he stopped before the man.

"My wife is about to give birth, but she is ill," responded the young man.

Zhang Guo Lao dismounted, then grasped his

Zhang Guo Lao is also a respected figure in other parts of the Far East. This 1915 print from Japan, where he is called Chokaro, shows how small he manages to make his white donkey. (Library of Congress)

THE BEST-DRESSED WIZARD

Shamans dressed in animal skins and tokens of sympathetic magic. As we see in contemporary Siberian shamanism, feathers, coins, ropes, ribbons, and disks of iron sewn into garments are common. Iron is associated with protection from spirits and with journeying to and within the otherworld – the shaman has a map on his garments to find home.

Early Greco-Roman magic emphasized purity for rituals so the garment specified was pure white linen, as worn by Egyptian priests. Merlin and his ilk tend to be depicted in blue robes deriving from Byzantine and Dark Ages depictions of St. Peter.

From Elizabethan times, wizards gained long robes and skullcaps as a reflection of fashion and as protective garments in the alchemical laboratory. The appearance of astrological symbols appears to be a continuation of medieval fashion but is actually coincidental. With the modern revival of ritual magic, influenced by depictions of wizards in earlier art, the two images combine to produce the robed acolyte and wizard that we see in Gandalf, with his practical robes and traveling cloak, and Dumbledore.

The wizard's staff is partly from the Roman historian Tacitus's description of the druids, but it was also practical for traveling. Of course, as well as the staff, wizards are depicted carrying daggers, swords, and similar items of particularly male symbolism.

A caricature of our idea of a wizard, with a beard, robes, black cat, alchemical jars and bottles, astrological symbols, and so on. (Library of Congress)

donkey with both hands and quickly folded it up and stuffed it away in a pouch on his belt.

"Take me to her," he commanded. "I'll see what I can do."

The young man took him inside, where a midwife sat beside the feverish woman about to give birth.

"I believe we could all use a drink," said Zhang Guo Lao. "To relax our nerves."

Pulling cups and a gourd filled with wine from his robes, he poured drinks for the man and the midwife, before taking a drink himself. Then, he mixed some herbs with the wine and gave it to the feverish woman, while moving his hands above her to re-balance her chi.

Immediately, the woman's fever broke, and in the next few minutes the baby was born with little pain for the mother.

That evening the new parents celebrated with the wizard. Eventually, Zhang Guo Lao stepped outside, took out a piece of folded parchment, and spat a remarkable stream of saliva onto it. The parchment swelled and unfolded, ballooning into a full-size donkey.

The young man came out just as Zhang Guo Lao was preparing to leave.

"How can we truly thank you for all you have done?" he asked as the wizard mounted his donkey.

"Don't tell the emperor I was here," Zhang Guo Lao laughed. Then he waved, touched his heels to the donkey's flanks and vanished.

A Second Imperial Summons

It was only a matter of time before news of the wizard's survival made it back to the emperor. He was furious but also recognized the wizard's valuable cleverness. He sent a letter to a mutual friend, named Fei Wu. Soon, Fei Wu and Zhang Guo Lao were sampling a vintage made with a new type of grape that the wizard had transported from a distant land.

"This is wonderful," said Fei Wu.

"Fit for the emperor himself," Zhang Guo Lao responded.

"Speaking of the emperor, I had a letter from him last week. He wondered if I might ask you about joining his …"

To Fei Wu's horror, his old friend suddenly choked on his wine. Unable to draw breath, the old wizard turned purple and dropped dead.

Fei Wu dropped to his knees, trying to revive his friend, but Zhang Guo Lao was already cold.

"I'm sorry!" shouted Fei Wu

"That's all right," Zhang Guo Lao said, "I forgive you."

With that, the old wizard sat up, and warmth and color returned to his skin.

"As long as I live and breathe I will never work for the emperor. Please tell him so when you reply to his letter."

The Emperor

Sometime later, the emperor invited the old wizard to his palace with promises of fine wine and assurances that he would not try to hire him. Zhang Guo Lao agreed.

A great feast was held, with a celebratory lion dance and displays by dancers, acrobats, and martial artists. The wine flowed like storm-filled rivers, and Zhang Guo Lao was impressed with its quality. Since the emperor had laid on such entertainments for him, Zhang Guo Lao decided to return the favor.

"You have shown great kindness to an old wizard. So, in return, perhaps your highness would like to see some magic?"

Zhang Guo Lao immediately vanished, to the gasps of everyone in the vast silk-draped hall. "Or not exactly see," the wizard's voice laughed from his seat at the table. A goblet of wine floated into the air to head-height, then tilted so that the wine vanished into an invisible mouth. With a chuckle, the wizard reappeared, still holding the goblet he had just drained. "A good party trick for a good party, eh?"

"A useful trick," the emperor said. "Imagine if our spies could do that, or our armies. We could defeat our enemies more easily."

"Let me show you another trick for dealing with potential enemies." With that, Zhang Guo Lao rose and went out into a private garden followed by the emperor and his guard. Zhang Guo Lao spread out his hands and began to whistle. In a matter of moments, numerous brightly colored birds fluttered down from their perches in the trees and settled on his outstretched arms.

"How does this deal with potential enemies?" the emperor asked.

"It's called making friends," said Zhang Guo Lao.

The Necromancer Yeh Fa Shan

Some years later, after Zhang Guo Lao had returned to his home, the emperor began to covet the old wizard's power for himself. Reasoning that the only person who could tell him how a wizard learned his skills was another wizard, the emperor called upon his court magician, a powerful necromancer named Yeh Fa Shan.

"Do you know how Zhang Guo Lao came to be so wise and powerful?" he asked.

"Yes, but I told you, I would die immediately, right here, for the sin of revealing heaven's secrets."

"What if I were to command you, on pain of death?"

"I dare not. Unless … If your highness will promise to go on a pilgrimage immediately afterwards, to ask Zhang Guo Lao to forgive you. If he does, I may be revived."

The emperor called in scribes to record his promise, and Fa Shan seemed satisfied.

"Very well, your highness. At the dawn of time, the cosmos was being forged from chaos. Then the spirit of a white bat …"

At these words, Fa Shan screamed, bleeding from his eyes, ears, nose, and mouth, and crumpled lifelessly to the floor. Horrified, the emperor ordered that his body be placed in safety but not buried, while he tried to persuade the great wizard to revive him.

The emperor traveled at once to Zhongtiao Shan and doffed his shoes and cap, humbling himself. Zhang Guo Lao invited the emperor into his little house, and offered him food and drink like any other visitor.

"I come to beg forgiveness," the emperor told him, "for forcing Fa Shan to speak of heaven's secrets. He should not have died, as I was the one to blame."

Zhang Guo Lao nodded slowly. "That young fellow always talked too much. If I didn't give him the odd scare, I fear he might divulge the secret

This Qing Dynasty (19th-century) painting, *The New Year Painting Of Zhang Xian*, depicts a scene from a story about the Lady Flower Stamen, in which Zhang uses a pellet bow to protect a group of children from a heavenly hound. Although he is always seen to be old, Zhang Guo Lao is seen as a bringer of sons and protector of children, and this image reflects that. It may also indicate that this element of his myth is drawn from the similarly-named Zhang Xian, an archer and philosopher of the 10th century, 200 years after Zhang Guo Lao's original time. (PD)

of the universe to anyone who asked. Come on then." He led the emperor outside, and they both mounted Zhang Guo Lao's donkey. In a flash, they dismounted at the palace.

The surprised courtiers immediately led the wizard and the emperor to Fa Shan's body. There, Zhang Guo Lao sprayed a stream of water from his mouth over the body, washing away the blood. Fa Shan sat up with a groan.

After that, Fa Shan promised to keep silent, while the emperor agreed that he would not seek out magical knowledge for himself. He had learned his lesson.

The Historical Zhang Guo Lao

Zhang Guo Lao is one of the legendary Eight Immortals of Taoist myth, all of whom are generally said to have been born in the Tang (AD 618–907) or Song (AD 960–1279) dynasties, even though many of their exploits are set centuries before that era. The stories of the Immortals came into their main form around the early 14th century.

Zhang Guo Lao was a historical figure, born sometime around the 670s, though he is recorded as having claimed to the Empress Wu Zetian around AD 700 to be hundreds of years old, and to have been the prime minister of the mythical Emperor Yao in the 23rd century BC.

The historical Zhang Guo Lao was a sort of priest who specialized in necromancy and alchemy, as well as a maker of herbal wines and a teacher of qigong, a combination of philosophy, medicine, and martial arts. In 735 he was made chief of the Imperial Academy in Hunan Province, a government position not far off being the Minister of Magic overseeing Hogwarts. The emperor at this time was Xuan Zhong, who reigned between AD 712 and 756.

Somewhere around 743, Zhang Guo Lao fell ill and returned home to Zhongtiao Shan, where he died around 745. A few days afterwards, a group of students from the Academy came to view his tomb and found his body gone. Perhaps this is one reason why he was credited with the abilities to recover from death and become invisible.

The Nameless Wizard

When the Arab world was centerd on Persia, there was a nameless wizard from the Maghreb in North Africa who was well-versed in the casting of spells and in exerting influences upon men's minds, as well as in the enchantment of items such as weapons and jewelry. He was sure that he could gain greater power by exploiting the djinni.

Djinni were said to be able to make themselves lighter than air, as solid as mountains, or as insubstantial as smoke. All secrets were known to them, and they could work magics that no wizard could, because they existed somewhere between the limits of man and god. This wizard managed to enslave one, binding it into the ring he wore on his right hand. He wasn't foolish enough to try to force it to do his bidding, but its immortal presence would protect him from danger.

Through his research, the wizard learned of an older and more powerful djinn, one whose power would make him almost omnipotent. It had taken years to discover the existence of the djinn and even longer to discover how and where to find it. The djinn had already been trapped and bound long ago, when the desert tribes still worshipped such spirits in rocks and oases.

Knowing where the djinn was and actually getting to it were two very different matters, however. By scrying in a jeweled orb, the wizard saw that the djinn was held inside a metal lamp, which was stored in an underground cave full of wondrous treasures. He also saw the bones of the many men who had tried to enter the cave through its hidden entrance. Few had got inside and none had come back out.

The wizard needed a master thief, but the only one he had ever worked with, a man called Qaseem, had died some years ago. However, Qaseem had left behind a son named Aladdin, and the wizard thought he might share many of his father's talents.

Aladdin and the Lamp

The wizard knew that the thief's wife had known little of her husband's background.

"Felicitations, my sister!" the wizard

said warmly, when he arrived in their village in China, at the far end of the Silk Road. "And this must be my nephew. My brother Qaseem spoke so highly of both of you." He sighed, sadly. "I had thought losing a brother was bad enough, but I can't imagine how terrible it must have been to lose a husband and father."

"It has been difficult," Qaseem's widow admitted. The wizard was pleased that she had accepted him as her brother-in-law. She had no reason to disbelieve her visitor, as it was clear that the visitor had genuinely known Qaseem quite well, and there were many bonds of brotherhood.

The wizard prepares to send Aladdin into the treasure cave in this Charles Folkard illustration from a 1917 publication of *The Arabian Nights,* which oddly spells the young hero's name as Alladin. (Hilary Morgan / Alamy)

"That is what I feared," he said. "I promised Qaseem that I would look after his family, and I will help set young Aladdin here up in business."

"What business?" asked the widow.

The wizard didn't want to mention either wizardry or thievery, so he said, "He will be a merchant of the finest rugs."

Trading in rugs was no difficulty for a sorcerer used to dealing with the acquisition of magical items, and as he got to know Aladdin, the wizard realized that Qaseem's influence had rubbed off on the boy, who was frequently in trouble. This made it easier for the wizard to suggest to him that they could acquire rather more working capital from a cave he knew about.

"It wouldn't be stealing," he told Aladdin. "This cave was filled with loot by a gang of bandits many years ago. There might even be a reward for recovering it."

"That sounds good," Aladdin agreed, "but the bandits must have booby-trapped it before they left."

"They did," the wizard admitted. "But I have this." He showed Aladdin the ring into which a djinn had been bound. "This will protect you."

"If you have the ring, why can't you just go?"

"Some of the tunnels are very small, and I won't fit. You will."

The entrance to the cave was under a trapdoor in the desert. The wizard charmed the trapdoor open, revealing a ladder. It was hard for him to part with the protective ring, even temporarily, but he knew it was necessary.

"Remember, this will protect you." The wizard hoped that was true, otherwise he would have lost his most valuable possession. "You will find a lamp," he told Aladdin, "small enough for you to carry back up the ladder, and the reward for it will make your mother rich."

The wizard lit a torch and gave it to Aladdin, who descended into the ominous darkness.

While he was gone, the wizard paced nervously. Aladdin had been down in the treasure cave for over an hour, and he was beginning to wonder if the boy was lost or had fallen victim to one of the deadly traps.

Using a scrying lens, he found Aladdin making his way back through the traps, with the lamp. Excited, he broke the top few rungs of the ladder. When

THE DJINN OF THE LAMP (OPPOSITE)

Although the Aladdin story comes from what is popularly called *The Arabian Nights*, and features an all Arab cast – with the exception of the emperor, whose ethnicity isn't specified – it has always been set in China. Historically, the Silk Road(s) were able to lead a traveler all the way from the Maghreb – the stretch of North Africa from Morocco to Libya – to China, or vice versa, so it's not that much of a stretch to have Persian or Maghrebi characters wandering around China.

Here, the nameless wizard sets the djinn of the lamp on Badroulbadour in her very Chinese mansion. In Islamic mythology, djinni are the third type of beings – along with humans and angels – who have free will, despite this one being enslaved.

he saw Aladdin's torch appear below, he warned the boy that the rungs had given way. Aladdin couldn't climb out while holding the lamp.

"Hand me the lamp, then grab my hand," the wizard told him.

Aladdin's face betrayed recognition that the wizard was trying to trick him. He tried to make it up on his own, but it was impossible, and he fell. The wizard was horrified to see both the lamp and his ring fall out of reach into the darkness. He had gambled and lost. Assuming that Aladdin could never have survived the fall, he left.

When he returned home, however, he was in for a shock. His familiar spirits and scrying lens showed that Aladdin had indeed survived the fall, and, worse, had managed to use the djinn in the ring to escape.

Since he no longer had the djinn from the ring to transport him magically, he had to ride to Aladdin's village along the Silk Road. By the time he got there, he found that Aladdin and his mother lived in a palace! Somehow, Aladdin had managed to marry the emperor's daughter, Princess Badroulbadour, and the wizard knew there was only one way that he could have risen to such prominence, with the aid of the djinn of the lamp.

The wizard cast a glamour upon himself, making him unrecognizable to his erstwhile sister-in-law. Knowing that the lamp with the djinn was ancient and probably dented in the fall, he introduced himself as a merchant.

"I trade in lamps. New for old; I will give you a new lamp in return for old ones in need of restoration."

Qaseem's widow was happy to hand over the battered lamp in return for a much better and brighter new one. Immediately the wizard summoned the djinn.

"I am your master now," he instructed it. "And you will obey me."

"I hear and obey," the djinn agreed.

The wizard knew that this djinn was reputed to be the most powerful ever, and decided to test its strength. The djinn of the ring had been able to transport people from place to place, so he commanded the djinn of the lamp, "Move this palace and everything in it to my home in the Maghreb."

Immediately, the djinn obeyed, and with a clap of his hands the palace was in the Maghreb, thousands of miles from Aladdin's village. The wizard was pleased and immediately began to have his household moved into the palace, while Badroulbadour and the other occupants of the palace were imprisoned. The wizard's happiness did not last long, however, as, within a day, Aladdin materialized at the palace gates, borne by the djinn of the ring. The wizard saw a chance to reclaim his property.

The djinn of the ring was powerful enough to make Aladdin invulnerable to the wizard's spells. The wizard set the djinn of the lamp on Aladdin, but the djinn of the ring intercepted it. While the two djinni struggled, Aladdin raced the wizard to the lamp. Being younger and fitter, Aladdin got there first, and immediately called off the djinn's attack.

"Carry us home!" he cried out.

The wizard returned to Aladdin's palace on foot once more. This time he used his glamour spell to disguise himself as an old wise woman.

Disguised as a lamp seller, the nameless wizard offers "new lamps for old" to the populace of Aladdin's Chinese village. (Mary Evans Picture Library)

Badroulbadour allowed the healer to stay in the palace lest anyone fall ill. The wizard had planned exactly that, and had brought along many poisons.

Unfortunately, the djinn of the lamp was not fooled, and it had no wish to be the servant of such a dangerous man again. It manifested itself to Aladdin, and told him who the healing woman really was. Aladdin immediately challenged her and broke the wizard's glamour. Before the wizard could react, he felt Aladdin's sword in his heart, and died there.

The History behind Aladdin and the Nameless Wizard

The story of Aladdin and the nameless wizard originates in *The 1001 Nights*, dating from the mid-16th century. The original has little to show that it is

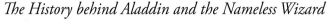

No British pantomime could hope to put on a spectacle to match this image for an 1888 burlesque version of Aladdin in the USA. For some reason the Djinn here takes his appearance from Faust's Mephistopheles – cross-fertilization between wizard legends! (Library of Congress)

located in China, but the setting has been brought out more in the pantomime that evolved from it in Britain, first performed in 1788. In the original tale there are two wizards: the master of the djinn and his elder brother.

Worldwide, a lot of people think the wizard is called Jafar, because that is the name given to him in the Disney cartoon film of *Aladdin*. However, Disney took that name – and some elements of his appearance and movement – from Conrad Veidt's character Jafar in the 1940 film *The Thief of Bagdad*. This Jafar was a version of the 8th-century Vizier Ja'far ibn Yahya.

In Britain, however, he is called Abanazar. This is the name he has had in the stage pantomime version since 1813. At the pantomime's first performance in 1788, the wizard character was still nameless, but he had already been combined from two brothers into a single character.

WIZARDS OF THE RENAISSANCE

Nicholas Flamel

Nicolas Flamel spent his days selling books from his stall in Paris. It wasn't much, just two feet per side, but it was all his, as was the house where his copyists produced his wares. It was a good, quiet life.

Then one night, an angel materialized in his bedroom. Despite its shining glory, his wife remained asleep beside him. The angel held out a leather tome and spoke.

"Behold this book and remember it well. At first you will understand nothing from it, but one day it will reveal great secrets too you."

Entranced, Flamel reached for the book, but the instant his fingers touched it, he was alone with his snoring wife.

A few weeks later, a stranger came to Flamel's book stall.

"I have something that might interest you," said the stranger, pulling out a book.

"I sell books," Flamel replied. "I don't buy them."

"Perhaps this will change your mind." He handed Flamel the leather tome that the angel had showed him. Flamel took it, pushed a purse into the man's hand without counting the money in it, then quickly closed his stall and went home to examine the book more thoroughly.

The book was old, bound in carved copper and edged with gold. The pages were made of thin bark, bound in groups of sevens. Every third page contained an indecipherable diagram. All Flamel could make out was the opening inscription in Greek, "This is the work of Abraham, Prince, Priest, Levite, Astrologer, Philosopher." There was also a warning that only priests and scribes could look upon the work without suffering ill; Flamel hoped that being a copyist and seller of manuscripts counted as being a scribe. The strangest thing, though, was the word "Marantha" which was repeated over and over on every page.

Flamel was no stranger to peculiar books. He had studied many alchemical texts over the years and had grown accustomed to the various codes and cyphers they used. Still,

A rather unflattering woodcut of Flamel, who appears to be wearing a large false beard. (Mary Evans Picture Library / Alamy)

NICOLAVS FLAMELLVS,
Pontisatensis,

53

A 14th-century manuscript illustration of alchemical equipment, allegedly by Nicolas Flamel himself, though it would be unusual for a writer and illustrator of the period to be the same person.

this book, which he called the *Book of Abraham*, was baffling.

He copied a few pages in the hope that one of his alchemist friends would recognize the writing, but none of them did. So he left the pages on display on his stall, hoping for the day a collector might recognize something.

For 21 years, the pages sat on his stall, and though no one could make sense of them, a few people recognized some of the words as Hebrew. Knowing that many of the Jews that had been persecuted in France had fled to Moorish Spain, Flamel made up his mind to go on pilgrimage. He told his friends that he was going to the shrine of Santiago de Compostella. Only to his wife, Pernelle, did he tell the truth. He was going to seek the kabbalistic scholars in Spain to see if they could translate the book.

The Wisdom of Spain

Flamel reached Spain safely, but the scholars he sought were understandably suspicious of French Christians. One night, as he rested at an inn, he started talking to a merchant from Boulogne over dinner.

"I may have to return home," Flamel said. "I had hoped to speak with some learned Jewish scholars, but …"

"Then it is fortunate you sat down here," the merchant said. "I know such a man, who lives in this very town. His name is Maestro Canches, and he lives only for his books."

They arranged to meet with Maestro Canches the next morning.

Maestro Canches proved a reluctant character; however, when Flamel mentioned the *Book of Abraham*, his eyes lit up.

"Abraham was a great master of those who study the Kabbala," said Maestro Canches. "This book disappeared centuries ago, but rumors say that it is secretly passed from hand to hand to the man whose destiny it is to receive it." Maestro Canches slumped. "I always dreamed of finding it, but now that I am dying …"

Flamel handed him the pages he had copied.

Trembling, Canches took the pages. The symbols, he explained, originated in ancient Chaldea. "But that is as much as I can tell from these pages."

"Then you must come back to Paris with me," Flamel urged, "and view the book."

"I am old," Canches protested, "and we Jews are barred from France."

"You are only a little older than me. And you can disguise yourself as I did."

Canches agreed, and they set off at once. As they traveled, the journey took its toll on Canches, who became weak and sick.

"We must reach your home soon," he told Flamel, "The *Book of Abraham* holds the secret by which darkness becomes light and flesh becomes spirit. I must know this secret before I die."

It was not to be. Maestro Canches died within the week, and Flamel returned home alone. Flamel now despaired of ever reading the book, but as he looked at it again, some of the words began to reveal their meaning. Although Maestro Canches had only deciphered a few pages, it had been enough to allow Flamel to begin learning the language.

The key!" he exclaimed to Pernelle, "I have the key to the cipher!"

Three years later, Nicolas Flamel stood at a desk in the back of his house, choking on the fumes emanating from a cauldron in which he had created a red powder he called projection powder.

With the *Book of Abraham* open before him, Flamel carefully placed the projection powder into a crucible, following the instructions from the book precisely. He poured in half a pound of quicksilver, and then had to flee to escape the fumes. When he returned, he found a cooling lump of pure silver. Excited, he continued with the experiment and soon refined the silver into gold. Flamel would never be poor again.

But there were further instructions in the *Book of Abraham*. Remembering Maestro Canche's eagerness to reach the book before he died, Flamel realized that the true aim of alchemy was not mere gold, but immortality.

Flamel died at the age of 80. His tomb was decorated with symbols that attracted alchemists from across Europe, but none learned anything from them. The *Book of Abraham* was bequeathed to Flamel's nephew.

Two hundred years later, a supposed descendant of Flamel appeared at the court of Louis XIII, where he turned lead shot into gold for the king's pistols. Cardinal de Richelieu was immediately interested and seized the book. Then, on a whim, the Cardinal had his men open Flamel's tomb. They found the tomb empty. Only then did Cardinal de Richelieu suspect the truth, but by then, Flamel had vanished once again.

The Historical Nicholas Flamel

Although Nicholas Flamel is probably best known today for his role in the story of Harry Potter, he really existed, having been born in the 1330s. He was a scrivener and bookseller, who ended up owning two shops in Paris, in the late 14th century. He certainly reached his 80s, which was rare for that era, and made a will two years before he died. Although Flamel's will shows generosity to the needy, his estate wasn't rich enough to imply he could make gold at will.

AGRIPPA AND THE DEMON (OPPOSITE)

It is often written that magical books are dangerous in one way or another, but even those that don't need to be chained down to keep them quiet can raise hell.

A magical grimoire is sometimes named an "Agrippa" after Heinrich Cornelius Agrippa, whose books were involved in a particularly spectacular example. Agrippa was an astrologer, soldier, student of Trithemius, and theological lawyer from Cologne, who lived between 1486 and 1535. He often got into theological arguments but wasn't seriously accused of wizardry until people studied his books later in the 16th century.

The best story that comes out of that revisionism tells us that Agrippa had once been working on a rite, unaware that one of his dinner guests was eavesdropping outside the room. When Agrippa left for a few minutes to walk his dog, the eavesdropper went to the book that Agrippa had been working with, started reading out bits and pieces, and inadvertently completed a spell to call up a demon. When Agrippa and his dog returned, they found the eavesdropper and the laboratory being mangled by the demon, which Agrippa then had to send back to where it came from.

There is also no evidence from the 15th century that he had any interest in alchemy beyond the fact that it was a popular subject for manuscripts, and so some texts had presumably passed through his shops.

It is no coincidence that the immortal version of Flamel was said to have turned up 200 years later, because that is when, thanks to a revived interest in alchemical historical texts, people started forging mediev___ or sale. An enterprising 17th-century bookseller trie___s of ___mel the Alchemist, most notably a piece entitled *Liv_____ues*. This is a book of symbolic designs allegedly com___ ___r a long-lost Parisian tomb, published in 1612 and ___sh a dozen years later. It was exposed in 1761 as having ___ne Eranaeus Orandus, the publisher of the book. The intro___ explains how Flamel learned about the Philosopher's Stone from the ___ *. of Abramelin the Mage*. In 1761, however, the historian Étienne François Villain demonstrated in his *Histoire Critique de Nicolas Flamel et Pernele sa Femme* that this had actually been made up by the publisher, P. Arnauld de la Chevalerie, who had written it himself.

Even Isaac Newton was taken in, believing Flamel to have been a legendary alchemist. In the 19th century, Victor Hugo and the composer Erik Satie were big fans of Flamel and referenced him in their work, while his great alchemical work was folded into the mythology of the Scottish rite of Freemasonry. His popularity has never waned since, as readers of J. K. Rowling, Umberto Eco, and Dan Brown can attest.

You can experience some of Flamel's alchemy for yourself. Aside from there being a street named after him, his last house, built in 1407, still stands at 51 rue de Montmorency in Paris, which now hosts a restaurant, the Auberge Nicolas Flamel. His tombstone, decorated with Christian saints, is in the Louvre.

Benvenuto Cellini

The boy Anselmo knew that when his uncle received his letter he would probably be dead, or worse. It was a pity, considering the effort his uncle had had to put into getting the boy his job as a sculptor's apprentice, but he knew he had to escape from Cellini's house.

Cellini hadn't been a bad master, just eccentric and given to rolling home drunk. He would often send him for things at all times of the night: a mirror, a mandragora root, chalk. But now things had changed. It began when he went to the door of Cellini's study with his supper and heard a mumbling that sounded like someone saying Mass. Then at 11 pm, surprise visitors arrived: a priest in a dirty surplice, Signor Andreas, a frequent tavern-going friend of the boy's master, and a stranger in fine clothes.

"Very good," the stranger said, looking at the apprentice. "He'll do."

LORENZO DE MEDICI

Lorenzo "the Magnificent" was a great patron of the arts as well as being a diplomat and politician. He supported da Vinci, Botticelli, and Michelangelo (who designed his tomb), and was also a poet and writer himself. He was also an avid collector of books and arcane texts, especially on astrology. He wrote down astrological spells in his own books, and owned a collection of ancient Greek ritual jewels that were known from an Arabic grimoire called the *Picatrix*, which is filled with incantations for summoning and binding demons, and drawing the influences of the planets into these gemstones for later use.

Lorenzo also had a distinctive ring, which he wore throughout his rule. It was said that he had used his knowledge found in those ancient books to summon a demon and bind it into the ring. His enemies tended to die under mysterious circumstances, slain by the demon at his command, and he was apparently able to influence minds from a distance.

In April 1492, the demon finally overpowered its master, breaking free from his ring and blasting the tower of the church of Santa Reparata with lightning. Lights materialized over the Medici family graves, and a bright star blazed in the heavens. After three nights of these portents, Lorenzo the Magnificent died, damned on his deathbed by the priest Girolamo Savonarola.

In truth, of course, bribery and alliances did his handiwork far better than demons. He did collect astrological grimoires and Hellenistic gemstones, but his writings were poetry, and he seems to have used the astrological books as inspiration for his similes. He wasn't even damned by Savonarola; according to letters written by those who visited his deathbed, he died relatively happy, blessed by the priest. The legend of the damnation comes from the diary of a copper smith named Masi, though it is true that there was a great storm in Florence around the time of Lorenzo's death.

A portrait of Lorenzo de Medici by Giorgio Vasari. (PRISMA ARCHIVO / Alamy)

In moments, all five of them were in the stranger's carriage en route to the Colosseum. There, they descended to the floor. The stranger and the priest lit torches, while Cellini drew a circle on the floor, muttering under his breath.

Then they constructed a bonfire, lit it, and sprinkled sweet-smelling herbs and powders onto it. The priest held up a pentacle and droned on in a language Anselmo couldn't identify. At first it seemed solemn, then, after an hour of chanting had passed, merely boring.

"They're here," the priest said at last, "filling the circle." He drew a new magical circle on the center of the floor. "I've bound them within this circle. What would you ask of them?"

Cellini stepped towards the circle. "When will I see my sweetheart again?" he asked. "It has been days since her abduction."

"They say in about a month."

Cellini turned to Anselmo. "Can you see anything, lad?" he asked. "Do you see the demons?"

Tired, hungry, and keen to please his master, Anselmo rolled his eyes and moaned theatrically. "Yes! I see four armed men trying to break into the circle from the other side!"

Anselmo smiled to himself as the four men frantically started throwing asafoetida on the bonfire to keep away the approaching fiends. He wondered

King Francis I of France visits Cellini's workshop. (Mary Evans/BeBa/Iberfoto)

A man working in metallurgy, goldsmithing and alchemy in the early 16th century would have had a furnace like the one in this 1530 woodcut. The portrait on the chimney hood may be Paracelsus, as it resembles his sepulchral stone. (Library of congress)

if they were all crazy or just drunk.

Then, suddenly, the quiet of the deserted Colosseum was broken by a tremendous fart. Signor Andreas blushed, while everyone else laughed.

"What a stink," Anselmo exclaimed. "The Devil himself couldn't match it."

Then priest stopped laughing. "Something has gone wrong," he whispered. He looked around wildly, then screamed and ran for the exit.

Confused, Anselmo and the other three men watched the priest run off. Then Cellini lit another torch, and swept it round the seats of the Colosseum.

Demons, glistening black and red, swarmed out of the floor and through the cracks in the walls. Everyone broke and ran. Anselmo followed after Cellini as he ran for the exit. They charged out into the street, pursued by a tide of demons that flowed like water down the narrow alley. Anselmo glanced behind him and saw them running along the walls and rooftops. They were all different colors, yellow, green, red, and blue. Some had horns; others were on fire. They had grotesque faces that resembled frogs, bats, and cats.

A horrible scream echoed down the street, a wail of pain and terror that was cut short. Anselmo recognized the voice. He knew the demons had caught Signor Andreas.

The rest of the chase passed in a blur of horror. Somehow Anselmo and Cellini made it back to their house and the demons gave up their pursuit.

Later that night the boy woke screaming and shaking. A cat was lying in the bed beside him. Hastily, he put the cat outside. He was about to go back to bed, when he saw a light in Cellini's study. He went to check on his master who was sitting with his back to the doorway. He spoke without turning around.

"Anselmo, I've been thinking, you're a damn good apprentice."

Then Cellini turned around and stared at Anselmo with a pair of cat eyes. "Well go on, what are you standing there for? Has the cat got your tongue?"

Swiftly, Anselmo ran up to his room and packed his belongings. He would run to the seminary and beg for sanctuary. From there he could seek penance and write to his uncle. He knew too much. He knew Cellini would come after him.

The Historical Benvenuto Cellini

This 16th-century excursion to the Colosseum at midnight may be the most famous account of a magical rite gone wrong and comes from the autobiography of self-confessed thief, braggart, brawler, alchemist, and necromancer Benvenuto Cellini.

Cellini was born in 1500. By profession he had been a goldsmith – an occupation frequently linked with alchemy at the time – musician, soldier, and sculptor. He had a habit of taking his female models as mistresses. It was the abduction of one of these women by her mother that prompted him to try to summon demons to find her.

He employed a priest whom he had met by chance in a tavern, along with the priest's strange friend, who burnt sweet-smelling herbs to encourage the spirits to turn up. Cellini had also brought along his 12-year-old servant boy, whose presence was important for several reasons. For dramatic purposes, he was an independent, non-magical witness, and having a pure innocent present showed a continuity of practice to Greco-Roman rituals. Asafoetida has been used for centuries as remedy for wind, so it is ironic that the demons are disturbed and the spell broken by a fart.

Cellini also claimed in his autobiography to have had a halo and to have had prophetic visions and angelic visitations throughout his life. He died in 1571.

In his job as a sculptor, Cellini teaches his assistant, Bernardino Manellini, with the aid of a figurine. (Liszt Collection / Alamy)

THE GOLDEN AGE WIZARDS

Francis Stewart, 5TH Earl of Bothwell

James VI of Scotland, now James I of England as well, had only been married for a few weeks to Anne, the sister of the king of Denmark, and now walls of water were battering the ship. Even the admiral of the Danish fleet escorting the royal couple was amazed by the ferocity of the storm.

"I've never seen the like," he said. "It's unnatural."

King James blanched, knowing what that meant. "You mean … witchcraft?"

"Witchcraft," the admiral confirmed grimly. "In Denmark we recently executed a coven who raised storms just like this."

Only a few miles away, a group of robed and cowled figures stared out to sea from a cliff-top field. Despite the black sea, black sky, and impenetrable sheets of rain and lightning, they all had their eyes fixed on the same distant spot, as if they could see the king's ship bumping and bouncing on the massive swells.

They chanted as they danced rhythmically, while a central figure in finer scarlet robes dipped a dagger into a goblet filled with thick red fluid. Around him, women with their hoods thrown back stretched their arms up to the skies, their hair flying loose around their heads. The figure in the scarlet robe turned, gathering the winds, and pushed out with his hands as if trying to shove someone off their feet.

At sea, a solid mass of spray slammed into the king's ship, ripping lines from the sail. Wooden tackle whirled across the deck, breaking bones as the ship lurched.

"Tack into the wind!" the Danish

King James VI of Scotland, notorious hater of witches, target of plots, and also James I of England. (North Wind Picture Archive / Alamy)

admiral shouted.

"We must make port at Leith," the king insisted.

"We'll never make it there. We have to turn away and head south."

"I am the king!"

"You are not my king. But your queen is my princess, and I will not endanger her."

Sullenly, the king fell silent.

On the cliff top, the robed figures lowered their arms.

"It is over," the man in scarlet said. "We have failed. The king lives."

The Witch Round-Up

In the little town of Tranent, in North Berwick, David Seaton was waiting for his maid to return. As dawn approached, he heard a window open in the kitchen. A shadowy figure was climbing through, and when he uncovered the lamp he was holding, he saw that it was his maid, Gillis Duncan.

"Where have you been at this hour?" he demanded. "Selling your healing salves?"

"No, no … I've been …" She trailed off, unable to think of a good excuse.

"Did you think I wouldn't notice? The potions, the midnight walks … I think we're going to have a little walk into town, Gillis."

The rest of the family had risen from their beds by now, so she had no choice but to go along with them as they frog-marched her to the jail at Tranent. A soldier met them there.

"What's going on here?"

"I think," said Seaton, "this woman is a witch."

It didn't take long before the king heard about this arrest and had Gillis brought before him. The king looked at her as if she was some new and particularly strange kind of insect. He was obsessed with witches and terrified of them.

"It will go easier on you," he told her, "if you tell me who else is in your coven."

"I dinna ken anything about any coven …"

"Then it's just coincidence that witchcraft from your town raised a storm to try to kill me and my bride?"

"Aye, I suppose so."

"Put her to the torture," the king told his men.

A few days later, the bleeding and broken Gillis was brought back.

"Talk to Agnes Sampson," she whispered.

So the king did exactly that. The elderly and well-respected Sampson was arrested and brought to Holyrood House. There, she was chained to the wall by the witch's bridle, a metal cage for the head with four iron spikes in the mouth. Denied sleep and kept with a noose around her neck, she eventually gave in.

"Who leads your coven?" the king demanded of her. "Who is your wizard?"

"The Devil himself," Agnes Sampson said. "The rightful prince. He told us that the king should be consumed at the request of the earl of Bothwell."

Soon others gave the same name. A man called Ritchie Graham came forward, confessing to having conspired with Bothwell to raise storms to kill the king.

The king was both horrified and delighted; he was horrified that such evil was so close to the court, but delighted that his enemy proved to be a known political rival. Bothwell was also the admiral of the king's fleet and so perfectly placed to have known where to raise storms to catch the king's ship.

"Arrest the earl of Bothwell," he told his guards.

Imprisonment

Francis Stewart, 5th Earl of Bothwell, was hurled roughly into a windowless cell in the heart of Edinburgh Castle. Still in his finest doublet, he slammed against the rough stone wall and dropped to the ground.

"I see James still knows how to be the perfect host," he shouted to his guards as they slammed the heavy door closed.

It wasn't long before the king himself descended into the bowels of the castle to question him through a grille in the door. It was the only opening, apart from a slot near the floor where dinner plates could be pushed through.

"Cousin …"

"Don't call me that, sorcerer," the king snapped. "You're no family of mine."

"The chancellor is behind this," Bothwell insisted. "He's jealous of my position, or fears for his."

"That you conspire … well, that's politics. But witchcraft, Bothwell? That's an abomination."

"This accusation is a greater abomination."

"We've rounded up all your witches. Those poor souls you've tempted, those souls you've bought … Aye, they'll be cleansed in the fire. The repentant will be strangled first, of course. As a mercy. You're going to burn too."

"Am I? Do you think even the most superstitious sheriff will believe the king's cousin is a wizard?"

"They will when the king confirms it. In three weeks, I promise you, you'll be back in hell where you came from."

Bothwell smiled slowly. "And what makes you think I'll be here in three weeks? If I am a wizard, what sort of cell do you think can hold the Devil prisoner?"

The king hurried away. He wasn't concerned about whether the authorities would believe Bothwell was a wizard; he had already forced them to convict over a hundred of his subservient witches.

A week later, he returned, talking through the grill in the door again. Bothwell, now in a rather dirty shirt, was still there.

"The cell seems to be holding you."

"Seems." Bothwell smiled, despite his imminent trial and execution. The king hurried away.

On the second week, the king returned again. Bothwell, filthy, was unbowed as he came to the grille.

"Remember, cousin, you're only king for life."

"Longer than you'll ever live," the king promised. "Next week, you'll be tried, sentenced, and executed."

"How do you execute the Devil?" Bothwell asked. The king ran out of the dungeon.

Three weeks after Bothwell had been thrown into the cell, the king led a troop of his most elite guards to escort his sorcerer cousin to his fate personally.

"Open the door," he ordered, giving the jailer the key.

The jailer hurriedly opened the door to the windowless cell for the first time since Bothwell had been incarcerated. It was empty.

"But …" the jailer paled. "He was there last night; he had his dinner …"

All the king could hear was the faintest echo of his cousin's mocking laughter.

That Christmas, the king was enjoying a feast in his private chambers when he heard a familiar voice.

"I told you a prison couldn't hold a wizard."

The king turned to see Bothwell standing in a corner, his hand on his sword. He was dressed as finely as he ever was.

"Did you come to kill me?"

"Maybe. Or maybe I came to try to get you to see sense." He stepped forward.

"Guards!" the king screamed.

Immediately the door burst open, and guards flooded in. It was too late, however, since Bothwell was gone, as mysteriously as he had arrived.

Gathering practitioners of the black arts was, oddly, a circumstance under which people from many different classes would work together with the same aims: to raise demons, alter the weather, and hold dubious revels. (Mary Evans Picture Library)

Magical Math

One day a youth neglecting his studies purchased a book on astrology in which he found a diagram that baffled him because the trigonometry required to understand it was not taught at his university. The book led him on an exploration of extant mathematical knowledge, and when he couldn't find the answer, he invented it. The year was 1664; the place was Stourbridge, near Cambridge, and the student was Isaac Newton.

Exploring God's world through science was seen as the highest duty of a hermetic or magician. Before Newton, mathematics was based on the Aristotelian and Platonian belief that perfect geometry existed only in the mind of God, and that earthly forms were an imperfect version of this.

The mathematics of circles and degrees of arc were required to understand the Greek model of the fixed heavens as interlocking crystal spheres. Their movement was precisely calculated to mathematical measurements, which translated into musical intervals, the music of the spheres. Geometry was also required in architecture, which was based on the ideal proportions of the human body. Hence the famous diagram of Vitruvian Man, which shows man and architecture reflecting one another, as in Hermes's central idea of "as above, so below." The value of pi was also thought to be magical because it could not be finitely calculated. The quest to turn lead into gold was expressed in terms of squaring the circle – having a square with the exact surface area as a circle held within its borders.

Before Arab mathematicians revealed it, Europe had no concept of the value 0, so this also attracted much magical significance when it was first introduced. The Chinese created the Lo Shu magic square in 650 BC – predating sudoku by millennia.

4 9 2
3 5 7
8 1 6

Here the lines of figures, horizontal, vertical, and diagonal, all add up to 15 (the number of days in ancient China's 24-month solar calendar).

Later, the precision of mathematics was transferred into the beliefs and practice of ritual magic in Greco-Roman times. For example, the Lo Shu square was associated with Saturn, and all the other planets had their own number squares that were used in incantations, which "geometers" would use in the creation of necromantic and other rituals.

The Historical Francis Stewart

In 1590, King James VI of Scotland married Princess Anne of Denmark, and during the return voyage their ships were assailed three times by deadly storms. The Danish authorities had recently had a witch-hunt against supposed witches who raised storms, and so perhaps it was their influence that began what became known as the North Berwick Witch Trials.

Overall, more than 100 people were arrested and 53 were executed. There was an added twist in that, as well as the usual type of suspects from the lower classes, a few respectable nobles, including the king's own cousin, Francis Stewart, 5th Earl of Bothwell, were implicated.

Bothwell and the king were grandsons of James V, and Bothwell was admiral of the king's fleet, but he was known to be envious of the throne. His father was suspected of having murdered the king's father, Lord Darnley. In fact, Bothwell's father, the fourth earl, had been legitimized as successor to the Scottish throne by both the pope and the king's mother, Queen Mary, who had been forced to abdicate in the king's favor. Worse still, Bothwell had been arrested only the previous year for conspiring to usurp the king at Holyrood, but his trial had been deferred on account of the family connection.

Even before the trials, it was written that Bothwell "had much traffic with witches and was himself an expert necromancer." That said, the king had so weighted the council of nobles against the accused to ensure convictions that the fact that Bothwell actually got away is pretty unusual. Only one other person was acquitted, a woman named Barbara Napier – at which point King James had the jury found guilty of contempt of court and forced a retrial with the "correct" verdict.

Bothwell was declared an outlaw three days after escaping Edinburgh Castle, the declaration saying he had "given himself ower altogidder in the hands of Satan." He really did come to visit the king in December of 1591, either to kill him or to explain himself.

In 1592, the Scottish Parliament stripped Bothwell of all titles and honors, and in response he brought 300 men to try to capture the king at Falkland Palace by decidedly non-wizardly means. This failed and he was forced to flee, hunted for months. In March of 1593 he mysteriously appeared in the king's bedroom, accompanied by armed men. This time, however, he had brought them for the theatrical gesture of laying their swords at the king's feet as a sign of loyalty. Amazingly, the king accepted this and pardoned him.

Bothwell didn't honor the pardon, however, and soon was engaged in battle with the king's forces, after which he converted to Roman Catholicism and went into exile, first in France and then Italy. He died in Naples in 1612.

While in exile, Bothwell wrote this letter to a French witchfinder:

> You Christians are treacherous and obstinate. When you have any strong desire, you depart from your master and have recourse to me; but when your desire is accomplished, you turn your back on me as your enemy, and you go back to your God, who being benign and merciful, pardons you and receives you willingly. But make me a promise, written and signed by your own hand, that you voluntarily renounce Christ and your baptism and promise that you will adhere and be with me to the day of judgment, and after that you will rejoice yourself with me to suffer eternal pains; and I will accomplish your desire.

Dr. John Dee (and Edward Kelley)

Dee sighed. His divinations for ancient Arthurian and Druidic treasure were not going well, and Queen Elizabeth was demanding more money to aid in the fight against France and Spain. On top of that, the expeditions to the Americas and Russia had not had much success either, despite all of his briefings and his charts. What he needed, he thought, was a man who could hear the voices of angels. Then together they could decode the secrets of the universe.

Dee's search led him to the town of Lancaster, where a man named Edward Kelley claimed that he could speak with spirits. Dee found him in the center of town, locked in the stocks for passing off fake coins and horoscopes.

"So you are the famous Edward Kelley," said Dee.

Kelly looked up at him as best he could. "Have you come to gloat?"

"No. I've come to see if you can really hear the angels."

"Their voices fill my head."

"With truth or lies, I wonder," said Dee.

"Angels cannot lie."

Dee laughed. "A bit of circular logic, perhaps, but well said. I have a proposition. If you agree to come and work for me, I will get you out of your current entanglement."

A Talk with Uriel

A few months later, Dee walked into his lab where Kelley was working.

"Today is the day, Kelley," Dee said, "I wish to speak with the angel, Uriel."

Kelley got to work on the preparations, fasting all morning and praying in the small chapel attached to their library. In the afternoon, Dee put him into a trance, and Kelley began dictating notes from the angel Uriel. While Kelley spoke in the strange language of the angels, Dee wrote every word down meticulously.

"One moment," Dee interrupted. "How should I spell that name?"

"A-N-N-I-E-L."

"That's what I thought you said," Dee muttered. "And it's wrong. It should have only one N, as an angel should know."

He looked at Kelley suspiciously. For months they had worked together like this, and Dee's journals were already filled with notes in Enochian, the language of the angels.

If Kelley were lying, the months would have been wasted.

"No," Dee muttered to himself. "You can't be lying to me. No one would be so foolish…"

DR. DEE IN HIS ELIZABETHAN LAB (OPPOSITE)

The image we have of an old wizard's study or laboratory in his tower, or his office in Hogwarts, is very much derived from contemporary illustrations of the environs of Dr. Dee and his ilk. The books, jars, sextants, stuffed crocodiles, and so on that we expect to see in such a room are exactly what you would have seen in Dee's home at Mortlake.

More accurately, it was Dee's mother's home in Mortlake, which Dee expanded, buying up all the neighboring houses so that he could expand his library and collection of esoteric artifacts – magic mirrors, globes made by Mercator, the Voynich Manuscript, etc – into them. In its day it was the biggest library in Europe.

The Trip to Krakow

One day, Kelly brought home a man named Albert Laski and introduced him to Dee. Laski was a noble from Krakow, and he suggested that Kelley and Dee join him at his estate when he returned there. He claimed to have worked for the king, and promised them full access to his vast library. It was a tempting offer to a book collector like Dee, and when an angel, speaking through Kelley, also urged him to go, he decided to make the trip.

When Dee and Kelley arrived in Krakow, they went directly to see King Stefan, to announce their arrival. When the king heard why the two men had come to Poland, he laughed.

"Laski," said King Stefan, "that bankrupt old blowhard? The only books he could show you are the ones holdings his bills at the local tavern."

Dee got a sinking feeling in his stomach and asked, "then there is no work for us either?"

"Not for Queen Elizabeth's spy, no." The king frowned. "Look, you're a respectable man, and your friend Kelley here is popular. Perhaps you should

This 19th-century engraving casts Dee and Kelley as necromancers conjuring the spirit of a woman at her grave, though this is not a type of magic with which the pair were actually involved. (Mary Evans/Interfoto)

THE WIZARD'S COURT

Rudolf II was a man ahead of his time, both fascinated by the natural world and convinced of the human ability to progress. His freethinking, Protestant court became a haven for the alchemical and magical cream of Europe and those persecuted as opponents of the Catholic worldview. The famous astronomers Tycho Brahe and Giordano Brunowere were visitors, as were John Dee and Edward Kelley. Kelley ended up imprisoned in the round tower of the castle of Prague, to this day known as "The Alchemists" Tower."

Rudolf was so keen on the allegorical images of alchemy that he planned the palace gardens as

Rudolf II, Holy Roman Emperor, alchemist, and math fan in a Flemish portrait. (The Art Collection / Alamy)

an alchemical journey through a landscape of bronze and other metal figures, streams, and allegorical set pieces. Sadly only part of it was completed before his death, but the plans remain.

Rudolf had a vast menagerie of beasts, including several lions. His favorite, Ottokar, is said to have shared its birthday with Rudolf and to have behaved quite tamely.

Rudolf died on January 20, 1612, three days after Ottokar. There were quite a few lions named Ottokar in Prague over the years, named after the 13th-century Bohemian King Ottokar, whose insignia was a two-tailed lion.

go to Prague Castle. King Rudolf is known to be a good friend to magicians."

"He must be a wise man," Dee said.

Prague Castle

The Holy Roman Emperor, Rudolf II, King of Hungary, Croatia, and Bohemia, indeed proved a good friend to Dee and Kelly. Dee had rarely met someone so interested in collecting magical esoterica and materials connected with the natural sciences, and his library was second to none. Upon their arrival, the king immediately found work for the two men.

One day, some weeks after their arrival, all three men were sitting in the library.

"This is a fascinating book," said Rudolf II, leafing through a thick volume filled with indecipherable text and drawings of unearthly plants. "How did you come by it?"

"It was given to me by a stranger," Dee said.

"And written by an angel," Kelley added. Dee glared.

"I should like to add it to my collection. How much would you want for it?"

"Consider it a gift," said Dee.

This time, it was Kelley who stared angrily.

A few days later, Dee and Kelley were speaking with the angel Uriel, when Uriel said, "You must combine your natures more completely. Suns and moons together. Each sun to the other moon."

Dee stopped writing and looked up in astonishment. "Are you suggesting we should trade wives?"

"Only then can our meetings continue," Uriel said through Kelley.

Dee closed the book he was writing in and brought Kelley out of his trance.

I fear," said Dee "that we have learned all that we can from Uriel. Tomorrow, I am returning to England."

"If you must," said Kelley, with a barely contained grin.

A few days later, as they packed their luggage onto a coach, a group of soldiers approached and surrounded them.

"Are you arresting us, or throwing us out?" Dee asked.

The captain replied, "You can go, Dee, but he stays here."

Dee opened his mouth to object, but then he remembered the suggestion to swap wives. He remembered Kelley's angels' misspelled words, and he remembered his initial meeting with Kelley, when he found him the stocks.

Dee said nothing as the guards dragged him away. It was only sometime later that Dee heard what happened to Kelley. It seemed that Kelley had been up to his old tricks of making fake gold coins. Unfortunately for him, the trick had managed to even fool the king. Kelley now spent his days locked in a tower, making counterfeit gold for the king.

The Historical John Dee

John Dee was a mathematician, cryptographer, and unofficial court philosopher to Queen Elizabeth I. He was never an official court magician because Britain viewed such a position as an unnecessary luxury and was unwilling to pay a wage for it.

At the time, Dee was viewed both as a bit of a wizard on political grounds – he changed sides more than once during religious upheavals on either side of the reign of "Bloody" Mary – and as Britain's first proper scientist and thinker. He taught Elizabeth I about alchemy, which was a subject of great interest to a monarch looking to replenish her coffers after many military campaigns. Although we view the Elizabethan period as a "golden age," it was actually a time of austerity, and treasure hunting was a national pastime. People believed that gold grew from the actions of the sun on the earth at the tropics – which was a major reason for founding colonies there – and Dee himself leased gold mines.

A 16th-century portrait of John Dee. The globe and compass reflect his early interest in mapmaking, as well as being his tools for astrology and casting of horoscopes. (Mary Evans Picture Library)

D.ᴿ DEE avoucheth his Stone is brought by Angelical Ministry.

Dee was first referred to as "Dr Dee" in a letter about his religious position during Mary's reign, but was actually awarded a doctorate later in life. He originally wanted to be a cartographer and was a friend of Mercator. In fact he provided the charts for the search for the fabled North West passage around the top of the Americas, but then turned to mathematics and cryptography. He believed that spirits and angels could help him decode the secrets of how the universe worked in a scientific manner.

Dee always had a reputation as a sorcerer; his London home was shunned by the local urchins for fear of magical reprisals. By careful purchase of surrounding property he built a space big enough to house the greatest library in England. None of it was catalogued, though it was said that Dee knew it so well that he could immediately lay hand on any volume in the whole edifice.

Dee's own view of magic, however, was less sensational and more practical. He insisted that a true magician was first and foremost a mathematician, and that his magic was based on the natural sciences, not superstition, which he despised. He anticipated Newton's discovery of gravity by imagining a magnetic-like force that bodies exerted on one another, and his finest contribution to magical literature was probably the *Monas Hieroglyphica*, which explained his view of the cosmos, and related it to a symbol he had created.

After his trip to the court of Rudolf II, Dee returned to England to find that his library had been looted. He was eventually given a post at Christ College at Manchester.

A wonderful, painted Mephistopheles on a poster for a 19th-century American stage production. (Library of Congress)

Johann Georg Faust

The Devil straightened his red-lined opera cloak and stepped into the private theatre box. God was already sitting there, quietly reading the program, his immaculate white suit glowing faintly in the dimness.

"Is this seat taken?" asked the Devil.

"Be my guest," God replied. His angelic smile beamed from his full-bearded face.

The devil took his seat, and the shadows thickened around it. "It's been a while," he said.

"And, if you don't mind me saying, you do seem to have rather come down in the world these days," replied God with a chuckle.

"I do mind," the Devil replied. "Popularity is a matter of marketing, and we don't all have your resources."

"Sssh, it's about to begin."

Slowly, the curtain rose on the theatre of the world, and the small audience looked down on a cluttered study …

A man in a velvet doctor's cap walked into the study. He sighed and looked around, his face revealing

FAUST BARGAINING WITH THE DEVIL (OPPOSITE)

The Devil has been portrayed in many different ways over the centuries, but has never been more dapper than when, in the form of Mephistopheles, he bargains with Faust – or Dr. Faustus, depending on which version you're reading – for his soul in return for money, women, success, and fame.

In fact, the Devil as a proactive figure who tempts humans to commit evil, and is portrayed in art as the source of evil, is, perhaps surprisingly, a 14th-century take on the character. Before that, he actually worked for God, as his jailer, rehabilitating souls in Hell. This is reflected in those versions of the Faust tale in which God and the Devil are not quite enemies at each other's throats all the time, but share a certain responsibility in their wager over Faust.

his frustration and boredom. He grabbed a book, flipped through it, and then tossed it aside. He did this again and again, his frustration mounting, until he opened one book and froze. He read intently, flipped a page, and read on.

Suddenly with a clap of thunder and a burst of light, the demon Mephistopheles appeared in the study. He introduced himself to Faust, and said that he had come with an offer from the Devil himself. Nearly limitless magical power for a term of 24 years, one year for each hour of each day, at the end of which, Hell would claim his soul. Mephistopheles wiggled his fingers and a contract appeared.

Faust read the contract quickly, then grabbed a quill and signed.

In an instant, the scene changed. Faust and Mephistopheles entered a tavern. The demon hammered a wooden tap into a bench, then turned the tap and released a stream of wine. The tavern-goers swiftly took advantage of it, got drunk and started brawling. During the fight, one man was decapitated, but managed to recover his head and reattach it. At this point, Faust and Mephistopheles made their exit, riding on a living barrel of wine.

In the next scene, the man and the demon stood on the street as a beautiful young woman passed. Faust looked on her with lust-filled eyes, while the demon arched his eyebrows and gave a knowing grin.

Up in the box, God turned his head and covered his eyes.

The Devil laughed. "You can't stop watching now. It's just getting interesting. That's the price of omniscience!

"That doesn't mean I have to enjoy it."

Back on stage, Faust used his dark magic to seduce the beautiful Gretchen, killing her mother and brother in the process. Later, when Gretchen gave birth to Faust's child, she drowned the baby in the river and was arrested for murder. Faust and Mephistopheles broke into the prison in order to free the girl, but she refused to be rescued, insisting that she must pay for the evil she had done.

Eventually, Gretchen was executed, but, because of her repentance, angels came and carried her soul up to heaven.

Carl Vogel Von Vogelstein depicts scenes from Goethe's version of Faust, with a much more demonic Mephistopheles, harkening to the serpent in the Garden of Eden, tempting the protagonist. (The Art Archive / Alamy)

"Typical," muttered the Devil.

From then on, the scenes became a blur of strange happenings and classical allusion. Faust and Mephistopheles traveled through time and the cosmos, on a search for ultimate beauty. Their journey eventually led them to classical Greece and Helen of Troy, where the pair got involved in the affairs of the ancient gods, heroes, and monsters.

Eventually, the 24 years had almost expired …

The Devil stirred in his seat. "It's all rather predictable, especially the *deus ex machina* to save the girl."

"Finding fault again," replied God. "Now that is predictable for you."

The two locked eyes.

"Faust is mine," hissed the Devil.

"We shall see," said God. "This story isn't over yet …"

THE HISTORICAL FAUST

Not only was there a historical Faust, there were actually two. Johann Faust was a German astrologer and physician probably born near Heidelberg in 1480, who was booted out of Ingolstadt in 1528 due to his homosexuality. Since he was already an astrologer, being persecuted for what were viewed as unnatural practices of another kind contributed to his reputation as a sorcerer.

This reputation was completed by the nearly contemporaneous existence of a Georg Faust, born in 1466 in Gelnhausen, who also had trouble in Heidelberg in 1506. He was a known conman and trickster who had been accused by the Church of trading with the Devil.

Whether the two Fausts were related is unknown, but they have since often been combined into a single figure named Johann Georg Faust. One or the other of them was killed in an explosion – a frequent cause of death among alchemists of the era – in 1548, his body so damaged that it was thought to have been torn apart by a demon.

Faust is said to have hosted dinner parties for his students at which spirits appeared and served 46 different courses with wine which mysteriously appeared from holes in a tavern. He reportedly cursed the unfriendly monks of a local convent with a poltergeist, conjured up the heroes of Greek mythology in front of his students to illustrate his lectures and burned off a clergyman's beard with arsenic.

Most famously he collaborated with the Devil in the form of Mephistopheles, with whom he signed a pact in his own blood, exchanging his soul for eternity to gain wisdom, riches, and success. The Faustian pact has been a trope of literature, legend, and culture ever since. Medieval texts are full of complex contracts to avoid trickery on the part of supernatural powers. One specifies that the spirit's gold "shall not be false nor of any material that can be cheapened or disappear into coal or anything of that kind."

A portrait of Faust at his studies in the normal way, rather than the supernatural way. (Library of Congress)

The Faust best known today is Goethe's 19th-century character. In Goethe's play, Faust the scholar laments that he has studied everything known, but is no cleverer than before, so he gives himself over to the Devil in order to understand the inner workings of nature. This Faust is torn between inadequacy and feeling equal to God in the use of his God-given reason. He is also held back by a lack of money, which would be understood in every era. Mephistopheles is also dissatisfied with his life, because all his attempts to do evil end in something good.

Goethe's Faust is saved by the intervention of his beloved Gretchen, but the original legend of 1589 doesn't end so happily. Faust refuses a priest's attempt to save him by saying Mass, because the Devil never broke his side of the bargain, so why should Faust? Faust's students cower as the whole house is rocked by an earthquake, there are terrible screams and Faust's corpse is found with its head on backwards.

THE MAGICAL LIBRARY

There are many famous magical books. Here are five of the best for the discerning wizard's bookshelves.

1. *Key of Solomon* (*Clavicula Solomonis*), supposedly written by the Old Testament king but probably early medieval. This book contains words for binding spirits and the names of angels for every hour and for every activity. There is even one, called Raziel, for libraries, as well as a minor demon by the name of Humots, whose job it is to "transport all manner of books for thy pleasure." Each spirit has a "sigil" or symbol, which the wizard can draw in order to summon him. It was printed in the *Sworn Book of Honorius* (14th century) and by 19th-century magician A. E. Waite as *The Ceremonial Book of Magic*.

2. Paracelsus, *De Libera Nymphis, Salamandris, Sylphis, Gnomibus, et Caeteris Spiritibus* (*The Book of Nymphs, Salamanders, Sylphs, Gnomes, and Other Spirits*). A guide to magical creatures that share the world with man and can become his friends, enemies, or servants. The nature of each group is related to the element in which they dwelt. Salamanders, living in fire, were a symbol for alchemical gold. Sylphs lived in the air and could be mistaken for people, except they were taller, paler, and thinner. A man and a sylph could marry and have a family, as could a man and a water-spirit. But he must be careful never to scold her near water, lest she disappear! Gnomes, being of the element earth, were trustworthy, dependable, and could show you buried treasure, but people had to be careful to pay their wages on time.

3. Cornelius Agrippa, *De Occulta Philosophia* (*On Occult Philosophy*). A work considered to be the medieval bestseller on magic, alchemy, and astrology. So popular was this book that an "Agrippa" became the name for a magical book in general. The other common name for a magical book was a grimoire, named after *The Grand Grimoire*.

4. Pope Honorius III, *The Grand Grimoire*. This is a set of four guides to summoning the Devil and demons. Honorius, who claimed to be the head of a European council of 811 wizards, launched a call to arms for wizards against persecution by the Church during the reign of Pope Gregory IX, insisting that the Church, not the wizards, was in league with Satan, as spirits would never work with anyone who was evil.

5. *The Shemhamphoras*. A Hebrew text taken from the words for the number 72. Using the numerical value of Hebrew letters, this book claimed to be a guide to finding 72 magical names of God. Oddly enough, the most secret one adds up to 811, the number of wizards in Honorius's council.

WIZARDS TODAY

Today we tell ourselves we're more enlightened than to believe in wizards, but we still follow their adventures in so many media: on TV, in movies, in books, and in games. What seems to matter to us is who's telling the story. In *The Thief of Baghdad* (1940) vizier, holy man, and scientist Ja'far Ibn Yahya of history has become the bad wizard Jafar, who magically blinds his king and steals his kingdom, all for love. This reminds us that even the greatest wizards of legend were, at the end of the day, people like ourselves who acted out of everyday motives, good, bad, or perhaps not so clear-cut.

What adult doesn't sympathize with Merlin imprisoned forever under a rock for his love of Nimue, to whom he offered his magical secrets? And what teenager wouldn't like the power of the Sorcerer's Apprentice, who was Goethe's before he was Disney's, to command buckets and mops to clean their room for them?

As Gandalf points out to Frodo, and Dumbledore to Harry Potter, and Obi Wan to Anakin Skywalker, with power comes responsibility. And as Terry Pratchett's Granny Weatherwax is fond of telling people, the real power of magic lies in knowing when not to use it and when common sense, courage and, as she puts it, "headology" will do just as well. After all, without our "magus" scientists of the past, who sometimes risked their lives to hand on to the next generation factual truths as well as the belief in a magical, endlessly fascinating universe underlying them, where would the physicists, chemists, mathematicians, and astronomers of the 21st century be today?

Sir Ian McKellen as literature's greatest wizard, Gandalf, in Peter Jackson's film version of *The Lord Of The Rings: The Fellowship Of The Ring.* (Photos 12 / Alamy)

Glossary

alchemy: The power to transform one object or substance into another, especially an ordinary metal into gold, using mysterious or inexplicable methods.

allegorical: Of or relating to a story in which fictional figures and events are used as symbols to represent spiritual or metaphysical truths or meanings.

caliph: The title given to a Muslim political ruler and Islamic religious leader who was seen as a successor to the Prophet Muhammad.

deus ex machina: Literally, the machine of god. Used to describe a literary device in which a difficult or seemingly impossible situation is contrived to be quickly and conveniently resolved, as if by the interference of a divine or supernatural being.

This illustration from the 1590s depicts Dee and a rather devilish-looking Edward Kelley working in their study. Kelley was later a popular alchemist in his own right. This is also an early source for the trope of wizards having stuffed crocodiles in their rooms, which is surprisingly common since! (Mary Evans Picture Library)

divination: The practice of predicting the future by interpreting signs, omens, or using special objects or powers.

djinn: A spirit in Arab and Islamic mythology that has supernatural powers, that lives on earth, and that can change forms.

druid: A member of the ancient Celtic religion who served as a priest. Druids were later seen as magicians or wizards.

glamour: An enchantment or magical spell.

grimoire: A magical book used by wizards, sorcerers, witches, and others that contains spells and invocations.

hermeticism: Alchemy or other mystical or occult practices, such as those attributed to Hermes.

Kabbala: Medieval Jewish mystical tradition in which Scripture is interpreted using ciphers.

magus: In the Near East, a wise or learned man who belonged to a class of priests. The term is also used to describe a sorcerer or magician.

necromancy: The practice of bringing back the dead in order to learn about and change the future; also, the practice of black magic or magic used towards evil ends.

pagan: Of or relating to a non-Christian and polytheistic religion, especially of ancient Rome or Greece, that is often associated with reverence for nature and earth.

pentacle: A magical object, such as an amulet or talisman, on which a pentagram—five-point star contained within a circle—is inscribed.

scry: To use a lens or other reflective surface to divine the future.

sigil: A written or illustrated sign or symbol that is said to have magical power.

transmutation: The complete change of a substance in appearance, form, or nature by natural or artificial means.

trope: A theme, expression, or literary device that is used commonly in a certain genre of writing, film, or other media.

vizier: A high-ranking official in the government of Muslim countries, usually used during the time of the Ottoman Empire.

FOR MORE INFORMATION

Arthurian Centre
Slaughterbridge, Camelford, Cornwall PL32 9TT
United Kingdom
+ 44 1840 213947
Website: http://www.arthur-online.co.uk
Visitors to the Arthurian Centre can view illustrations, paintings, manuscripts, artifacts, and more that are related to the various legends of King Arthur, the Knights of the Round Table, and Merlin.

Fantasy Museum
c/o Mist Valley
234 East Market Street, Suite 1
Harrisonburg, VA 22801
(800) 949-5673
Website: http://fantasymuseum.com
The Fantasy Museum strives to engage the public with the fantasy genre by examining related literature, art, and gaming. Interactive exhibits and games online educate visitors on the history of magic, fantasy, and mythology and acquaint them with the many inhabitants including wizards of magical realms.

Institute for Contemporary Shamanic Studies (ICSS)
2106 33 Avenue SW
P.O. Box 86114 Marda Loop
Calgary, AB T2T 6B7
Canada
(416) 603-4913

Website: http://icss.org
Striving to share shamanic teachings, the ICSS offers classes, seminars, and shamanic guidance and healing. Various programs are open to the public.

International Alchemy Guild
P.O. Box 22309
Sacramento, CA 95822
Website: http://alchemyguild.memberlodge.org
Members of the Alchemy Guild independently seek to continue the traditions of past alchemists by performing and sharing research and techniques with each other and the public. The guild is also involved in the creation of the first alchemy museum and laboratory in the United States.

Museum of Alchemists and Magicians of Old Prague
Jansky vrsek 8, Prague 1
Czech Republic
+ 420 257 224 508
Website: http://www.muzeumpovesti.cz/en
Visitors to the Museum of Alchemists and Magicians of Old Prague can tour the home of Edward Kelley and visit the alchemy lab in which he worked. Texts on display and interactive exhibits allow visitors to better understand the role of alchemy in history and literature.

Science Fiction and Fantasy Writers of America (SFWA)
PO Box 3238
Enfield, CT 06083
Website: http://www.sfwa.org
SFWA supports writers and readers of the science fiction and fantasy genres. Recommended reading lists, sample lessons, and information for new and experienced writers in the genre are offered on the organization's website.

SF Canada
P.O. Box 95
Alberta Beach, AB T0E 0A0
Canada

Website: http://northbynotwest.com/sfcanada-wp
SF Canada supports Canadian writers of speculative fiction—
fantasy, horror, science fiction, and related genres—by organizing
writing groups and meetings and publicizing works by its
members.

WEBSITES
Because of the changing nature of Internet links, Rosen Publishing has
developed an online list of websites related to the subject of this book.
This site is updated regularly. Please use this link to access this list:

http://www.rosenlinks.com/HERO/Wiz

FOR FURTHER READING

Ardrey, Adam. *Finding Merlin: The Truth Behind the Legend of the Great Arthurian Mage*. Woodstock, NY: The Overlook Press, 2013.

Curran, Robert. *The Wizards' Handbook: An Essential Guide to Wizards, Sorcerers, and Magicians and Their Magic*. Hauppage, NY: Barron's, 2011.

Davies, Owen. *Grimoires: A History of Magic Books*. New York, NY: Oxford University Press, 2010.

Davies, Owen. *Magic: A Very Short Introduction*. New York, NY: Oxford University Press, 2012.

DuQuette, Lon Milo. *Enochian Vision Magick: An Introduction and Practical Guide to the Magick of Dr. John Dee and Edward Kelley*. York Beach, ME: Weiser Books, 2008.

Farrell, Joseph P. *The Philosopher's Stone: Alchemy and the Secret Research for Exotic Matter*. Port Townsend, WA: Feral House, 2009.

Halsall, Guy. *Worlds of Arthur: Facts and Fictions of the Dark Ages*. Oxford, UK: Oxford University Press, 2013.

Hauck, Dennis William. *Sorcerer's Stone: A Beginner's Guide to Alchemy*. Sacramento, CA: Crucible Books, 2013.

Kieckhefer, Richard. *Magic in the Middle Ages.* Cambridge, UK: Cambridge University Press, 2014.

Klaassen, Frank. *The Transformation of Magic: Illicit Learned Magic in the Later Middle Ages and Renaissance.* University Park, PA: The Pennsylvania State University Press, 2013.

Knight, Gareth. *A History of White Magic.* Cheltenham, UK: Skylight Press, 2011.

Lawrence-Mathers, Anne, and Carolina Escobar-Vargas. *Magic and Medieval Society.* New York, NY: Routledge, 2014.

Lawrence-Mathers, Anne. *The True History of Merlin the Magician.* New Haven, CT: Yale University Press, 2012.

Michelet, Jules. *Witchcraft, Sorcery and Superstition: The Classic Study of Medieval Hexes and Spell-Casting.* New York, NY: Skyhorse, 2014.

Page, Sophie. *Magic in the Cloister: Pious Motives, Illicit Interests, and Occult Approaches to the Medieval Universe.* University Park, PA: The Pennsylvania University Press, 2013.

Principe, Lawrence M. *The Secrets of Alchemy.* Chicago, IL: The University of Chicago Press, 2013.

Redgrove, H. Stanley. *Alchemy: Ancient and Modern.* London, UK: Forgotten Books, 2014.

Rider, Catherine. *Magic and Religion in Medieval England.* London, UK: Reaktion Books, 2012.

Roob, Alexander. *Alchemy & Mysticism.* New York, NY: Taschen, 2014.

Sherman, Aubrey. *Wizards: The Myths, Legends, and Lore.* Avon, MA: F + W Media, 2014.

Index

DATE DUE